THE COOLING BOARD

AN ELDON TRULY MYSTERY

BY ALAN HICKENBOTTOM

Lat45 Press | Hood River, Oregon

This is a work of fiction. Any resemblance to real events or persons, living or dead, is entirely coincidental.

ISBN: 979-8-9917219-2-9

Contact: thecoolingboard@gmail.com

Design by Dardi Troen

1

THE SOUND OF her bedroom door closing with a slight click. Her father's footsteps receding down the hall. Signals she could come back to herself. Back from the place she went when her door would creak open after her mom had passed out for the evening. To the the lingering smell of Scotch she thought *Done*. The word shown in her mind like a roadside billboard. *Done. Done, here.* Quietly she made her way to the basement and filled her pack. She was pretty sure where Brittany, Kyle and mama would be on this May night. Rachel had disappeared before. But this time she told herself she wasn't coming back. She padded out the terrace door, the one farthest from her parents room, in her stocking feet. Halfway down the curving driveway she stopped to lace up her boots, shouldered the pack and headed out of the West Hills down towards the city.

2

A FEW WEEKS later, with June at its best behavior, a properly upscale and average Japanese sedan turned off Broadway Blvd, glided down the underground parking ramp and stopped at the valet station. Matt Taylor handed over his keys and walked to the elevator. Behind him a low rumble descended the ramp and Matt turned as an immaculate, not average 74 Chevy Impala pulled in behind his car. An old blues tune poured out as the door opened, then silent as the key was turned. As the driver stepped from the car, he was not quite what Matt expected. White guy, six two, with a military bearing in country western formal. Blue blue-jeans, shined cowboy boots, a tweed sport coat over a button-down white shirt topped off with a Stetson. The Chevy driver passed his keys to the valet, a manila folder in his other hand. Matt held the elevator door for him.

"Floor?," Matt asked.

"Thirty five," the cowboy replied. "Thanks."

"Don't hear enough Little Walter in this town," Matt said.

"Hmm?," the cowboy said as he watched the floors count by.

"Little Walter. *Hate to see you go,* right?," replied Matt.

"Indeed. Nice catch," the cowboy said, his eyes staying on the floor count.

Matt looked down at the manila folder and caught a glimpse of the label. A name he knew, or thought he knew. The elevator slid to a stop as a vaguely sultry computer voice announced floor twenty-one. The doors slid open and Matt stepped off the elevator. The Chevy driver paid no attention.

The same voice announced floor thirty-five and the elevator doors parted, whispering something like money as Eldon Truly entered the lobby of Barton, Strand and Conner. Double high windows to the far wall with downtown and the river in the foreground. Beyond that, the Cascade Range foothills crowned by Mt Hood. In front of the windows was a long, low reception desk - a single piece of old growth Douglas fir - a slab of red-blond wood twenty feet long, tight-grained and knot free. The walls on either side held large abstract paintings and hand woven rugs covered the white oak floors, each probably costing more than his car.

Seated at the desk were, according to the name plaques, Abby and Emily. No need for last names. There was this Abby and there was this Emily and then there were all the others. Both looked to be in their mid-twenties, professional dress, little make-up or jewelry. But like an old friend used to say, you gotta car with a motor like that, you don't need fancy paint.

The mountain, the art work and the rugs along with Abby and Emily competed for Eldon's attention. Abby won so he walked to her end of the fallen giant, removing his hat.

"Good morning, may we help you?," she ask, pushing a lock of honey blond hair behind a sea shell ear.

"Morning, ma'am. Here to see Mr. Barton. We have a nine o'clock."

He was laying the cowboy thing on a bit thick. But the clients seemed to like it.

"Oh yes, he told us to expect you. He's tied up for a moment. In the meantime, may I get you some coffee? It's the firm's own roast."

Of course it was, he thought.

"Yes ma'am, that would be fine. Thank you. Black, please."

As she walked from her desk he thought that some women couldn't get the hang of high heels; unsure, sort of stooping and teetering as they walked. Abby wasn't that kind.

She returned with the coffee, the mug embossed with the firm's logo. Abby smiled and he smiled back and they exchanged the look that very attractive people give each other. Then her look said don't bother and she returned to her desk.

"I bet you get that second cup of coffee," Betty had said that morning. She was Eldon's business manager and always ran the Google, Facebook, Linked In routine on any new clients.

"C'mon, Betty. Its his daughter. I won't even have time to sit down."

It was a wager, a little game they played, Betty and Eldon. If it was an important client, or more precisely, one who thought themselves very important, the amount of time waiting told you how much trouble the client was in. So, while Jeffrey Barton's ego was never in doubt, they were talking about his daughter, an only child. The bet was always the same - a Powell's gift card for Betty, new guitar strings for Eldon.

"C'mon, Eldon," she said. "Rich white man like Jeffrey Barton? You better hope they've got some nice coffee table books in the lobby."

Eldon wandered to the art work, a hulking abstract that took up most of the wall. The style seemed familiar and he peered at the title card. Indeed, Eldon had been hired by the artist a couple of years ago. A few smaller pieces had been lifted by a jilted lover. And seeing that the artist was married, and the lover an inconvenient age and gender, Eldon got the call.

After a bit, Eldon eased into one of the leather couches, placing his hat beside him. He picked up one of those nice picture books, figuring he could hit Powell's bookstore on the way back to the office for Betty's gift card. Finally, towards the middle of his second cup, Jeffrey Barton strode into the lobby with a smile and an open hand.

"So sorry to keep you waiting, Mr. Truly," he said. Eldon marveled at how one could be apologetic and condescending at the same time.

"Eldon's fine," he replied, offering his own. They did the manly handshake dance, firm but not too firm, Eldon letting the client squeeze just a bit harder.

"I trust you received the information?," Jeffrey said. "I thought it might save us some time."

He placed a hand in the small of Eldon's back, gesturing down the hall with the other. As they left the lobby Eldon glanced at his watch. He wondered if he should get two gift cards.

From Jeffrey's corner office, there was same view of Mt Hood to the east with the imposing arch of the Fremont Bridge in the foreground and the cathedral spires of the St Johns Bridge beyond that from the north facing window. In the distance was the rounded summit of Mt St Helens.

"Nice view, Mr. Barton. Not sure I'd get anything done."

"Indeed, Eldon," as Jeffrey turned to the view. I do find myself looking out the window from time to time. "Thankfully, Abby and Emily keep me on task."

I'll bet, Eldon thought.

Jeffrey motioned to a pair of facing leather couches on the right, under a wall filled with photos and plaques.

"Please excuse me for just a moment. One last call," he said.

He picked up the phone, some sleek Danish thing.

"Abby, would you get Mr. Avery at the senator's office on the line?"

This seemed all part of the act and Eldon assumed his role was to admire the contents of the wall. The photos showed either the powerful and civic Jeffrey Barton or the active and manly Jeffrey Barton often with people Eldon recognized, sports stars, politicians, and others with a look that said, by god, you should recognize them.

Well, that was interesting. It was one of the manly and active photos. Five people squeezed on the front seat of a whitewater raft, the guide rowing from the rear seat in mid-rapid, the boat tipping into a wave, sparkling droplets frozen around them. It was one of those photos they take from the bank and try to sell you at the pull out. A girl, maybe twelve, sat between two couples, the men on either side of her, two women on the outside. Jeffrey Barton, composed as always, had his arm around an attractive if strained brunette with a look that said she needed a drink. The girl was beaming, laughing, in a bear hug with the other couple. The woman, a red head, was wearing a huge grin. But its was the man that caught his attention. Eldon sat down as Jeffrey hung up the phone and smiled. One of those smiles where you just use your mouth.

"Sorry, Eldon," joining him on the opposing couch. "Thanks for coming downtown today. I thought we should meet, at least this once. See if you have any questions. You've had a chance to look at the folder?"

"Yes, thanks," said Eldon. He went through the usual list; the last time they'd seen her, any friends she might have contact with, maybe a boyfriend, was she seeing a therapist, and more difficult questions about drugs or alcohol or prostitution - all received with a pleasant but blank stare.

"Maybe you should talk with my wife, Genny, But no, nothing that I know of."

Christ, you'd think he'd lost his car keys, Eldon thought. No, he'd be more upset.

Jeffrey's cell phone purred once and he slid it from his jacket.

Eldon flipped through the folder again as Jeffrey tapped away. Physical information - shoulder length brown hair, light olive skin and hazel eyes like her mother, average height and weight, no known tattoos or piercings - along with a set of recent pictures. Rachel alone and with some friends or her mother and father. Jeffrey, always dashing, and her mother Genny, stunning if a bit tight around the gills. Rachel certainly looked normal and happy but Eldon had seen enough beautiful photos of deeply fucked up units to know better. They probably didn't get her a new car or made her take out the garbage. These people spend seventeen years building perfectly spoiled monsters, then wonder why they turn on them. Still, she didn't look like the type and he knew better than to ask. There were a lot of reasons.

Jeffrey signed off his call and turned to Eldon,

"Sorry, where were we?"

"How long's she been gone, Mr. Barton?"

"About six weeks, Eldon. She's been gone before but never for this long. Her mother is very worried. I've called my friends at the Portland Police Department, of course. But one more runaway doesn't mean much. They just add her to the list."

"Any idea where she might be?," Eldon said.

"We're pretty sure she's living on the street with a few others. From what I understand, runaways will form, I don't know, families, to look out for each other. She texts her mother once in a while - never the same phone, of course. But, it seems like she and the group are traveling the I5 corridor with the usual stops - Ashland, Eugene, Portland, Seattle."

Jeffrey stood and looked out the north window. The neighborhood beyond downtown, Old Town, was a mix of 19th and early 20th century buildings and new apartment buildings along with a couple of construction cranes.

"With Rose Festival coming up, with the crowds and the money, she might even be in Old Town right now," Jeffrey said.

Eldon pushed himself off the low couch and walked to the wall. He nodded towards the rafting picture.

"This guy a friend of yours, Mr. Barton?"

"In a manner of speaking. That's Matthew Taylor and his wife Peg. He works in this building as a matter of fact."

"Yeah, I know. Rode the elevator with him," he said. Eldon remembered how Mr. Taylor's eyes had lit on the folder.

"Interesting," Jeffrey replied. "You know, Eldon, you might keep tabs on Mr. Taylor. He and Rachel, and his wife Peg, were quite close at one time."

"Why don't you ask him? I thought you were friends."

"A valid question," Jeffrey said. He looked down and picked a piece of lint from his pants then gazed out the window.

"Like any long time relationship, we've had our ups and downs," he said. "Our last 'down' happened just before my family and I moved to D.C. for a few years. Not long after that photo was taken, in fact." Jeffrey turned back to the window. "Really haven't spoken much since."

Jeffrey Barton walked to his desk and pressed a button on his phone and a moment later Abby entered the office.

"Thank you for coming, Eldon. Please let me know if you need anything. I've arranged for your expenses. Abby, please make sure Mr. Truly gets the envelope I left at the front desk."

With that, the audience concluded.

Eldon decided he didn't like his client very much but they didn't pay him for that.

3

JUST SHY OF noon, Matt Taylor walked out of his building and into that lovely day. His favorite lunch spot was about six blocks, across Burnside Avenue, a busy east west boulevard that divides downtown from Old Town; office workers and shoppers from tourists, hipsters and homeless along with a smattering of low key drug dealers. Although Old Town had gotten a little less rough in Portland's rush to gentrification it didn't hurt to keep your eyes open once the street signs went from SW to NW. On the other side of Burnside at Fourth Ave sat the Chinatown gate, two ten-foot fu-dogs flanking an arch. And just beyond was Good Taste Restaurant, a relic from when this really was Chinatown, before it all moved to the east side.

Hanging in the window, heads still attached, was a small flock of roasted ducks, along with sides of shining pork ribs and tenderloins. He pushed open the door, held up one finger and the waitress, the same one for the last 15 years, who he was pretty sure still didn't speak English, pointed him to a table and sent his usual order to the kitchen. He was still thinking about this morning, the guy with the Chevy. It made some sense. Jeffrey Barton's office was on the thirty-fifth floor and he had heard that his daughter Rachel was on the street again. Only this time she hadn't been home for a while. All second hand; rumors among the

Portland downtown business crowd. Until he saw the cowboy and the folder: R. Barton. So maybe after lunch he'd take a stroll through Old Town. Too nice a day anyway, the June rains were scheduled to return tomorrow.

A smile to the waitress, an extra tip on the bill and Matt left the restaurant. But instead of turning left, back towards downtown, Matt turned right, farther into Old Town. Just another anonymous office guy out for a noontime stroll. He wandered through the blocks, the center of Portland's burgeoning homeless population, passing discrete drug deals, tents on the sidewalk, panhandlers and people passed out in the doorways of closed store fronts. All of this interspersed with new condo buildings and fifty dollar a plate restaurants. Thinking back on it later, he wasn't sure why he had turned into the alley off Flanders, maybe a voice he recognized. But as he passed between the bruised walls and a rank dumpster the June day turned to dusk.

There was a girl, *Rachel?*, and a man with a knife. "Hey!" Matt said, and the man, and his knife turned towards him. The girl used the distraction to run for the far end of the alley. He vaguely noted that fact but lost that train of thought when the man came toward him. Matt backed up against the greasy wall, time doing a crazy slowing down thing. Matt wondered what it would feel like, the knife going in. And then a person, a voice, appeared to his right. A calm, steady voice and Matt thought, Well that's interesting, there's someone else here but I better just keep an eye on that knife, and the calm voice said, "Why don't you just put the knife down and move along, friend."

"You're next," said the man, and lunged.

Matt thought, Well there it is, I'm stabbed. Except he wasn't. An arm, a hand, shot out and grabbed the man's wrist and twisted the knife free and Matt watched as the man who'd been holding the knife took one two three punches and was down. Matt's savior pulled the man into a doorway and quickly, almost gently, laid him out. Just another passed out drunk in Old Town, the man with the calm voice said, mostly to himself, as he bent and scooped up the knife. He turned to Matt who stood, blinking, like with a flashbulb pop and said, "Let's move on, nice and easy," as he touched Matt's elbow. Almost as an afterthought, the man pulled out his phone and took a photo of the prostrate form. "One more thing," the man said and looked through the wallet before sliding it back in the punk's pocket.

Out of the alley, in the light, time resumed its normal pace and they reentered the bright June day and Matt thought, Its the cowboy, the guy from the garage. After a couple blocks the cowboy casually dropped the knife, rattling, into a storm drain. A couple more blocks and Matt, still shaking, said, "I really owe you. Can I, can I buy you a beer or something? There's a good pub a couple of blocks away."

"Sure," the man said. "Looks to me you could use one."

Dark and woody with books lining the walls, The Tugboat sat on a side street just off Broadway, in a seam between downtown and Old Town. The guy behind the bar had a waxed mustache and a plaid shirt; the Portland uniform. He looked to be in his late twenties, probably with a PhD in some obscure discipline.

"What'll it be gentlemen," his heavily tattooed arms spread wide across the bar.

"IPA," Matt replied. "Please." He also had both hands also on the bar, but more like he was steadying himself against a light swell. The bartender looked at the cowboy.

"Same, thanks," he said.

With the pints on the bar, the bartender returned to his Proust. Resisting the urge to lift the glass with both hands, Matt drained half the pint.

"Glad you came along when you did," Matt said. "Not sure how that was going to end. Well, no, I know exactly how that was going to end. Nicely done, though. Not your first time, I assume."

"Yeah well, I grew up in a tough town."

"Where was that?"

"Memphis. Lived with my grandmother after my parents died. Well, it wasn't that bad but she didn't live in a great neighborhood and a new kid in town made a nice target. Plus some time in the service."

"I like your taste in music, by the way. That was you in the garage this morning, right? The Little Walter was a nice touch. Oh, shit, hey, I don't even know your name. Matt," he said and offered his hand.

"Eldon. Pleased to meet you. And thanks for the beer."

"You pressed the floor for Jeffrey Barton's firm this morning," Matt said. "That folder had his daughter's name on it."

"He did say you two were acquainted."

"I grew up with him. Can't really say we're friends. Our fathers were sort of in business together. But you can't say, right? Client privilege and all that?"

"Yeah, something like that," Eldon said. "Don't supposed you've seen her though?"

Neither one of them mentioned that it was Rachel in the doorway. But maybe Eldon hadn't seen her. He was having trouble putting the order of things together. Either way, he wasn't sure what to think of Eldon yet, or rather someone who worked for Jeffrey. The bartender looked over, Matt nodded, Eldon shook his head, most of his glass still in front of him.

"Haven't seen her in years," Matt replied. "So, do you play? I mean Memphis and all that."

"Yeah, I play a little guitar. You?"

"Oh, I play a some harp. You know, the Little Walter thing."

Looking at his watch, Eldon got up. "I better get moving. You OK?"

"Yeah, I'm all right."

Eldon pulled out his wallet and handed Matt a card.

"I'm always looking for someone to jam with," Eldon said, "if you're game."

"Yeah, that'd be cool," Matt handed Eldon his own.

They shook again and Eldon disappeared into the glare of the open door, June sunshine spilling in. The door shut and Matt was left in the dim light, the crazy glow of the afternoon fading with Eldon's departure. He caught the bartender's eye for another.

Why hadn't he told Eldon about the girl, Rachel, in the alley? He seemed like a decent guy. But he wasn't so sure about his employer.

The door opened again. Dust motes swirled in the light and Matt half hoped it was the return of Eldon. But no, it was three men in primary color polo shirts tucked neatly into creased khaki slacks. They took the other end of the bar. Out of town businessmen just in from the airport from the look of it. No meetings until morning and time to start drinking.

Matt, his sanctuary violated, looked into his beer, willing them to go away. But on they went, in something close to Matt's working language, about tenant improvements and cost per square foot and vacancy rates until one of them mentioned Mary's Club.

"Yeah, its Portland's oldest strip club," the guy in the salmon polo said. Like that made it OK. Like they were going to a museum or something. "Let's go after dinner," he said.

Mary's was three doors down from the Tugboat. Matt hadn't been there since college. But as he listened to them prattle on, commercial real estate brokers or some such, it felt like a great idea even as his gut clenched a bit at the crossing. To be seen darting from the Tugboat, on a side street at least, into Mary's Club, on Broadway proper, did have its dangers. Matt could just hear it. *Yeah, Bob saw him stumble out of the Tugboat into Mary's last Tuesday. Looked like he was tanked. I knew he and Peg were having trouble.*

Matt thought of Sniper Alley, a boulevard in Sarajevo that got its name during the Balkan War. Crossing it left you open to Serbian snipers and going to market or getting to work could get you killed. OK, so that was a bit much and go he would, three beers and nearly stabbed all the permission he needed. Matt had turned into that alley after lunch, the day had gotten weird and he wasn't ready to unweird it.

He paid the bill, pushed off from the bar and opened the door, winching at the brightness. Infants believe if they close their eyes no one can see them and Matt squinted, staring at his feet as he navigated the seventy feet to Mary's door. It opened to the low thump of dance music while his nose met with fryer grease, stale beer and cheap perfume. The darkness resolved to a purple pink light. Pretty much as he had remembered it, Mary's Club was a narrow, deep room with the bar opposite the door sharing the same long wall as the narrow stage and, just beyond that, a tiny dressing room, more like a booth. The rest of the club was filled with empty four tops and two tops, the chairs facing the stage. On the walls, among Blazers and Timbers posters, was the usual assortment of beer signs, liquor specials and photos of the girls.

Having safely made the crossing, Matt slid onto a barstool and exhaled. Since it was Tuesday afternoon, Mary's was empty but for the bartender and a woman sitting at the bar, scribbling in a notebook. The bartender was forty-ish and bored, leaning against the bar back with her arms crossed. At the bar was a young woman who, now that he looked, was wearing nothing but a men's dress shirt. Pretty much the same blue button-down shirt Matt was wearing, it seemed. Well, that would be a dancer and Matt thought he'd like to sit next to her but left an empty seat between them.

The bartender tipped her head and looked at him, eyebrows up.

"PBR, please," Matt said.

She unfolded her arms and reached for a glass. Turning back, she tossed out a coaster, sat the beer down and returned to guarding her dissatisfaction. Taking the first pull on his beer, the place didn't have the va-va-voom he'd imagined, but yeah, it was a weekday afternoon. To his right, the dancer was writing in a well worn spiral notebook and Matt took a glance. Notes, drawings with lots of right angles and figures, dollars maybe. He was trying to imagine what a stripper would need all those numbers for when, satisfied with her conclusion, she turned.

"Hey there. Need a dance?"

"Uh, no, thanks," Matt said. "Just a beer for now."

He could see her reflection in the back bar mirror. Maybe twenty five with short blond hair. Slim, maybe tall, even lanky. A bra and, another side glance, panties under that open dress shirt. Nothing fancy but there was the shimmer, that refraction of light from the breasts of a young woman like those whistles only a dog can hear, something maybe only men could see, the reaction about the same.

"Ok, well just let me know," she said and turned back to her notebook.

Matt was thinking more about that dance. The song changed to something more familiar. That's funny, he thought, and tipped his glass to the bartender.

"Nice pick," he said.

"Don't look at me." She grunted and looked at the dancer. "I hate this shit."

"Oh yeah, that's mine," the dancer said. "Darcy here doesn't think much of the blues."

The bartender let a tiny smile escape, soon caught and returned.

"Its funny. That's the second time today," Matt said.

The dancer looked up and her shirt fell open. It confused him and Matt wished she wouldn't do that.

"Excuse me?," she said.

"Oh, um, I heard some Little Walter this morning. Same song in fact. My day's been weird ever since."

"Oh," she replied and returned to her notebook, tapping the pencil against her forehead, scratching some more notes. He noticed she was left handed with trim nails, no polish. A nail on her right hand was black, like when you catch it in a door, or with a hammer.

Little Walter faded out, followed by the Be Good Tanya's version of In My Time of Dying. Mildly smitten over the blues thing, Matt thought, let's see if this girl knows her stuff.

"Great pick," he said. "I wonder if they got the rights from Zeppelin."

She took the bait. "Fuckers," she replied. "I mean yeah, you gotta love Zepplin, but trying to put their names on the old blues stuff was bullshit. At least the Stones gave credit. Well, most of the time," she said.

She scooted into the seat next to his, "Amy," she said and held out her hand. Her shirt fell open again and he mentally counted the cash in his wallet. "Um, Matt," he said, offering his own and refocusing, well, not quite like a man's hand but she was no wilting violet and the conversation went on to favorite artists; him, besides Little Walter, Howlin' Wolf and Muddy, of course; her, Big Mama Thornton, and there's a girl from Kansas City, Samantha Fish. They both agreed on The Who, sucks, and loved that kid from Austin, Gary Clark, Jr, The Black Keys and Jack White. He asked about her taste in music, no offense, but you seem kind of young for this stuff, and her reply, growing up on a commune outside of Eugene, that's what all the hippies listened to when they weren't listening to The Dead, which she couldn't stand, by the way. You?, she said. Here, I'm a Portlander, he said with some kind of apology attached to it since that wasn't nearly as cool as growing up on commune but they were both native Oregonians, she said, and that was something. Did they play? Well yeah, he said, some blues harp, not quite middling, and her, well not really playing, but she could sing a little bit and so it went and, yes Darcy, another PBR would be just great, thank you.

They'd moved onto local bands when the light shifted in the mirror. Laughing nervously, the three guys from the Tugboat took seats at the stage. Must be far from home, he thought. Jumped right past the expense account dinner to dessert.

"Hey, Darce," Amy said. "Where's Sheila?"

"Doesn't come in til two," Darcy replied.

"Guess I'm up," she said and stashed her notebook behind the bar. Touching his shoulder as she brushed past him.

"Nice talking to you. Come have seat if you want."

He caught her scent; no perfume, just her, like she'd just gotten out of the shower. Another tumbler fell.

On the stage, Amy said, How you guys all doing today?, while the men's chairs pulled close. The music started and her eyes went somewhere else as her body found the rhythm. She knows what she's doing, Matt thought, wiping his mouth with his hand. Looking and not looking as he tried to ignore the laughing and manly chatter of the out-of-towners, he was about to join them at the stage when he caught his reflection sandwiched between the whisky bottles in the back-bar mirror. A drunk guy in a strip joint on a weekday afternoon. That broke the spell and it was time to go. He caught Darcy's eye and put two twenties on the bar.

"Hey, Darcy. Can you make sure Amy gets one of these? Thanks."

"Sure," she said, somewhat defrosted. "Take it easy."

A bit unsteady this time, Matt pushed back from his second bar of the afternoon. He stole a last look at Amy, in just her panties now, in a languorous swirl down the pole. She caught his eye and smiled.

"Hey Matt, nice to meet you. Come back some time. I'll play some more blues."

"Uh, yeah," his stammer covered by the music, "that would be great. Take care."

On the shitty side of a day drunk, he emerged on to the boulevard, the sidewalk and street busy with day end traffic. He blinked in the late afternoon sun. Too bright and too many beers. Still burning the last of the adrenaline and a little stunned by Amy, Matt prayed he didn't run into anyone he knew as he followed the lines in the sidewalk, straight and true up Broadway, like a guide to his building.

4

THEY MET BEHIND a boarded-up super market off SE Division and 122nd surrounded by graffiti and garbage. Weeds poking up through the seams and cracks in the pavement. A breeze down the low canyon of the alley swirled paper, leaves and discarded chip bags as he peeled off a few twenties from the roll and pressed them into Annabelle's sweaty palm. She was coming down from a two day meth bender, which included three or four car break-ins or maybe five or six.

"Thanks man," she said, sniffling and shuffling off down the alley to a waiting late nineties Toyota with cracked windshield and a crushed-in door. As the sound of the old Corolla, clearly needing some exhaust work, faded away he sat in his car and fired up the laptops just to see what he could see. The first was password protected and tossed aside. But the other two came right up and the man, mid-thirties with dark hair and dark eyes in jeans and a hoodie, smiled to himself. An Assistant DA had once said something about an animalistic charisma during final arguments. The man looked through the email account and browser history. It wasn't the real reason he wanted the units but he usually came up with some easy pickings - Amazon accounts with all the data loaded up, including credit card info. But even if the card data wasn't there he'd use one of the wallets or purses the Annabelles of the world brought with them. God, he thought, These people were fucking stupid. He'd pay them maybe a couple of hundred dollars for the stuff, and then order, acquire or transfer ten times that. But that was OK. That left him alone to gather the rewards. But even this wasn't the real reason for using the pilfered laptops. No, for that he'd head across town to a nondescript coffee shop, one with an open internet connection. Settling in at snug table, where someone couldn't look over his shoulder, he'd take a few minutes downloading a bit of software. The Tor browser was a favorite of paranoids, tech heads and, in this case, Cory Stalmer, who was neither. It was written to hide the user by bouncing traffic through and around and over anonymous routers and firewalls, leaping and hopping around the world finally landing at its final destination - a server located in Russia or Latvia or Nigeria or southeast Portland. Since English was the universal language and the Dark Web didn't really encourage chit chat, he was never sure but then he never cared either. And he'd thought about using bitcoin or one of the other crypto currencies but as long as he was supplied with a steady stream of freshly stolen credit cards, it didn't really seem necessary. He placed the orders he needed to fill his stock, with a couple of extras because once in while, but less than you'd think, they really were thieves and they'd take the credit card number but never actually ship anything. But most were pretty dependable. Some even had customer service links and live chat for questions. And over the next couple of days the small packages would begin to arrive at UPS stores and post offices in the suburbs. They were never in his name, of course. He'd give one of his junkies a couple of hundred dollars to go out set them up in their name and bring back the key. If they only knew, Cory said to himself as he pulled into the strip mall in Newberg, 20 miles outside of Portland, where he kept his one permanent PO box. With a hello to the middle aged woman behind the counter, he'd turn the key and remove the contents. Once or twice a year, in the PO box with the bills and the plain brown packages would be an envelope, return address St Louis. The notes were pretty much the same. *My dear brother, I love you and Jesus loves you but you know I can't take this money. I could put it to good use but because I know where it comes from my conscious won't allow it. I pray for the time you let the Holy Spirit into your heart. In Jesus name, Timothy.* And Cory did what he always did. He pulled out the bills, a roll of $20s and $100s and tossed the note in the garbage, walking out with a smile and a, *Have a nice day,* to the woman behind the shipping counter. Heroin, fentanyl, cocaine, roofies - it was all so easy. Even better, half the suppliers would pre-package it for street sale. The shit would be in and out of Cory's hands in an afternoon. After dropping a couple packages with bogus return addresses and no fingerprints in the outgoing mail slot, he headed for his car. If he didn't scoot, he was going to be late for the last meeting.

Cory didn't fuck up very often as his line of work had a very low tolerance for mistakes. But he'd been unlucky and popped for a DUI and a few weeks ago had started the court mandated drunk driving class; four weeks of lectures, statistics and gruesome accident photos. He'd noticed her at the first meeting. As he surveyed the other dozen or so morose souls, it was about what he had expected; a mix of earnest first timers among grizzled veterans itching for a break so they could get a smoke and sneak some Jack Daniels into their soda. But there was another, across the room, with a tilt to her shoulders that caught his attention. He could pick out the vulnerable ones, the usable ones - to fuck or to pimp or maybe mule for him. Usually they came from a lower social strata. With her light brown hair, neatly pulled back and fastened with a simple silver barrette, silk scarf and what even Cory could tell was a very expensive purse, this one clearly breathed more rarified air. But he could pick up the scared woodland creature vibe a mile away. He emptied his face and came back with what might be called 'open and warm.' Over the course of the afternoon caught her eye a couple of times, with a very shy smile. And when she held his eye that extra second, he knew he was close. She sat in the hallway during break, among the uncomfortable plastic chairs and vending machines. Apparently ignoring her, he pressed a selection and dug in his pockets. Nothing.

"Well, shit," he said quietly.

"I'm sorry," she said pulling up her hand bag, "Do you need some change?"

"Hey, thanks," he said. "I'll pay you back. I guess we'll be seeing each other for the next few weeks. I'm Cory," he said with a smile.

"Oh, hi," she said, returning his smile. "Nice to meet you. I'm Genny."

5

MATT MADE HIS way back to the office, hoping to miss Stacy, the receptionist.

"Oh hey, Matt! There you are. Your 4pm just called. She's on her way. Lucky her flight was late."

Oh shit, he'd forgotten. He was showing a vacant floor to a potential client. If it had been someone local, he would have begged off. Apologies and an undescribed schedule conflict. But she'd flown up from Silicon Valley. Another software company in search of cheaper rents and the Portland vibe.

They'd met at Higgins for lunch a couple of weeks ago to go over her needs. Well, her company needs anyway. They'd shared a bottle of wine and she laughed at his jokes and touched his arm when she needed to make a point, which seemed pretty often. And now he had a few options to show her. Like today. And now she was here. He ran to the bathroom, brushed his teeth and pushed his hair around and met her in the lobby. The chemistry returned as they rode the elevator to the 28th floor. They exited the elevator and walked to the floor to ceiling windows, Portland spread out beneath them. Who knows, maybe it was the smell of fear and adrenaline and sex he was giving off, but the next thing he knew, she had him pushed up against the glass, her tongue in his mouth.

"Sorry," she said. "We haven't got much time. I need to get back to the airport." The strangest day ever collapsed to her lips and he searched with his own tongue until another picture, another evening, appeared in his mind.

Matt and Peg had helped organize a fundraiser for one of her causes. He lost track which. It was around midnight and Matt just wanted to go home and sleep. But there was a bunch of food left over and Peg thought it was a shame to toss it. So, Matt's objections ignored, they had loaded the food in the car and headed for Old Town, crowded with the young bridge and tunnel crowd. They had come to the scary city to get drunk, do drugs and find one of their tribe to have sex with. But at the MAX station under the Burnside bridge, they had found what Peg was looking for. Here slept perhaps fifty homeless people, their sleeping bags and shopping carts lined up along the back retaining wall out of the drizzle. Peg pulled the Lexus to a stop.

"Perfect," she said. "these guys will take this stuff."

Matt is nearly apoplectic with fear as she got out. Peg told him to get a grip and a pulled a box of food from the trunk. Matt is sure they will be pulled down by the rabble, beaten, raped and left for dead. Peg just laughed.

"C'mon, you chicken. They're harmless, just a bunch of people trying to get some sleep."

A few of them stirred awake, curious about what's coming towards them. What they see is a vision, a beautiful woman, dressed for Saturday night, floating towards them bearing boxes.

"Hey guys," she called out. "Anybody hungry?," dropping a box at the feet of a small group. More are waking now, stirring from their bags.

"Wow, really? For us?"

"Yeah, well we were at this party and there was a bunch of leftover food. Seemed a shame to waste it," replies Peg. "Hey Matt, drop a couple boxes down at the other end."

"No fucking way!," a guy yells from his pile of blankets and filthy clothes. There is a call and response down the line and the swapping begins, rueben traded for ham and Swiss, like some Mad Max version of the school lunchroom as Peg and Matt pointed the Lexus up Broadway toward home.

Matt groaned as he gently pushed her away. "I'm, I'm sorry. I can't," lamely wriggling his left hand in front of her. She looked at his ring and back at him with a half smile.

"Mm," she said, "that's cool. But I need to see the server room before I go."

Back in his office Matt figured that deal was gone which was a bummer as they had been trying to lease that floor for a year. And thank God Peg had something tonight. Book group, maybe.

But the next morning an email showed up from her in his inbox. No note, the signed lease attached.

6

AMY FINISHED HER set with a wink and scooped up her clothes and tips. One of the guys pulled out a ten and slid it across the stage.

"Not one more?," he asked.

"Sheila's up," she said. "She'll take good care of you. I'll be back," she said and gave him his very own wink.

Sheila, raven haired and tatted up, came out of the tiny changing room. She was curvier than Amy with pierced nipples and a Goth thing going. The Midwesterners were mildly freaked out. They drank their beers and scooted their chairs up, scraping the floor.

"Hey sweetie, all yours," Amy said. Pulling her close, she whispered in Sheila's ear, "The guy on the right," she said. "He's the tipper."

Sheila looked his way and gently took Amy's earlobe in her teeth. They played this good girl, bad girl thing sometimes. Two wolves steering the herd into a dead end canyon. Darcy, for her part, made sure the cattle never got thirsty. The guy on the right breathed through his mouth and shifted in his seat. There's a feminist thing about stripping and exploitation and there's definitely something to that. But today Amy, Sheila and Darcy might argue about who was getting exploited. As Sheila went to work, Amy fished her notebook from out behind the bar.

"Hey Darcy," she said, "hand me the calculator, would ya?"

Tapping the keys, she thought, yeah, another couple hundred bucks ought to do it. The door opened behind her and Darcy brightened.

"Hey buddy," she said as a Stetson plopped down in the seat next to Amy. Eldon slid into the next seat down.

"Hey E, what's up?," Amy said. "Aren't you going to sit next to me?"

"Naw, I don't sit next to younger women without much for clothes on. Someone might get the wrong idea."

Amy rolled her eyes as Darcy slid a beer over to Eldon.

"Thanks, Darcy," he said and turned to Amy. "Watcha' working on?"

"Just figuring how much I need to finish that project, the one in Gladstone. A couple of more lap dances ought to do it."

"I thought one of those guys over might be one of them," she said. "But their wives probably do the bills." Amy held up an imaginary credit card bill and put her best housewife face on. "Hey hon', what's Mary's Club?"

"You do that pretty well, sweetheart," Eldon said. "Maybe one of these guys will take you out of here."

"Fuck off," she replied and punched him in the arm.

"There was another guy in here earlier," Eldon said. "Kind of like those guys," angling his head toward the stage. "You know, a middle-aged, corporate type."

"Oh yeah, Matt," Amy said. "A blues fan. Second time today, or something, the guy said. Something about Little Walter."

"Yep, that's him," said Eldon.

"Kinda jumpy, though," Darcy piped up. Eldon always made her chatty. "But a good tipper," Darcy said and pushed the twenty across the bar to Amy.

"Sweet," Amy said, tucking the bill in the back of her notebook. "Oh, I get it. On a hot case, Eldon? Jealous wife?"

"Naw, runaway teen. The daughter of a friend of the guy, or sort of friend. Haven't gotten it all figured out yet. I suspect his nerves were from more than seeing you naked. Although," he said looking straight ahead," that might do it," which earned him another punch to the arm. He told them about the alley and the guy with the knife.

"And I think the girl, the one I'm looking for, was her. The guy was pretty cagey about it though. This guy and my client have some history."

Sheila ended her set with a smattering of applause.

"Gotta go," Amy said.

"Hey Amy," he said. "If that guy comes by again, would you let me know?"

"Sure," she said. And with a peck on Eldon's cheek she made her way to the stage.

7

IT WAS LATER that afternoon and Sheila still had two songs left. Amy sat at the bar. She put her notebook aside and flipped through the local alt weekly; muckraking journalism framed by alternative health, beer and cannabis ads. A picture caught her eye. The woman, maybe a barista or a shop clerk, was attacking, punching, kicking what looked like the Pillsbury Doughboy's homeless brother. Behind them stood a group of cheering women in a martial arts or dance school with the headline: Michelin Man Gets His. With a tongue in cheek, those silly girls tone, the story was about a women's self defense class that taught, not technique, but pure, reptilian-brain aggression. They were supposed to tap into that part of them that said it will be you or me. In the beginning, the male volunteers wore some padded clothes, maybe a helmet. But as women were spun up in a form of bloodthirsty method acting, every brutal father, grabbing boss, or worse, came back and the volunteers kept getting their noses broken and ribs cracked. So they added more padding, more layers and by the time they were finished, he looked like the tire guy, if he slept out of doors. But it was the woman in the picture that took Amy back. The woman's face was knotted and vicious. But in her eyes was something else. A dead eyed calm.

* * *

In every child parent relationship, there's a point where roles reverse and the child becomes the parent. For most children it happens as parents pass middle age. Through a combination of undiagnosed mental illness and weekly ingestion of psychedelics her mother made the handoff somewhere around Amy's fifteenth birthday. They lived west of Eugene in the Coast Range at a place called Hyla Farm with some twenty or so free spirits. While they never referred to it this way, so nineteen sixties, most would call it a hippie commune. But there were enough other cogent and sentient beings at the Hyla Farm that Amy and her mother got on well enough. Probably the most sentient was Mike. He was around the same age as Amy's mom and about a hundred years wiser. Amy sometimes wondered, hoped, that he might be her father. She thought he wondered this too. Mike and Amy's mom went back a ways in Oregon's hippie scene. LSD and mushrooms were plentiful and memories were hazy so it was possible if unlikely since he mostly thought Amy's mom was crazy, which she was. Mike taught Amy to split wood, build a fire, shoot a gun, skin a deer. And that last summer, when the older boys were teasing her, pushing her around, he taught her to box. He put together a makeshift bag in the barn and over a couple weeks he taught her how to keep her elbows in, keep her punches short and efficient, none of that round house stuff. Of course, once they found out about it, the lessons were one more thing to ride her about. One bloody nose later, a crimson smear across the boy's face, was all it took for the teasing to stop. But the path through that memory, her crooked smile and Mike's wink as he helped the boy to his feet, always led to another one, like walking into a dank house from a sunny day.

They got all kinds at the commune. Most folks were cool. Once in while, someone showed up for reasons other than raw milk, sand candles and macramé. The farm grew some legendary bud. Marijuana wasn't legal yet and Oregon's weed culture was still dark around the edges. Darrell came out of that shadow. He had the kind of skinny you get from too much time on the road, the sinew from time in jail. Pretty much everyone was welcome as long as they did chores and minded their own business. But Mike, always reciting Shakespeare, mentioned something about Cassius. Lean and hungry, he said.

It was Amy's day to gather firewood and there was a downed alder snag half way along the road that followed the creek to the county highway. Darrell said he was hitching out that day and would walk with her. Frankly she was glad to see him go, even if she'd have to listen to his bullshit on the walk with how much weed he'd smoked, how many Dead shows he'd seen. The dirt track, an overgrown logging road, followed the creek, to their left, out of the clearing. The sounds of chickens, chopping wood, and someone plinking away on a 12-string faded as they left the clearing with the pull cart. The alder, big leaf maple and Douglas fir of the coastal rain forest closed around them and after ten minutes or so, the track steepened and came against a rock buttress where the path took a hard right along the base. It was here the day before, trunk rounds and cut branches strewn about, that Mike and some others had sawn the fallen tree. Tired from the walk, Amy and Darrell shared the water bottle and went to edge of the ravine for a look. Somewhere above, up through the canopy, was the sun, and a few glimpses of blue. It was a sea of forest and they were swimming, or somehow suspended, floating in it, all dappled sun and a million shades of green. When Amy was little she believed that the parts of your eyes that saw green, the cones and rods that fired the signal, would tire, that the sheer volume of light and tone would overwhelm the circuit. Below, maybe thirty feet to the bottom, the creek danced and jumbled in the rocks, barely visible through the thicket. Darrell sucked his teeth but was otherwise quiet. In fact, he hadn't said much since they left the clearing and for that she was grateful.

As they turned and set to work, the firs swayed in a slight breeze, still warm in the early fall and they took their time filling the cart. A raven called and another answered as Amy paused to look for late season berries, maybe the first chanterelles, and picked some miner's lettuce for dinner. Behind her Darrell said, Well shit, and she turned to see his pack spilled out onto the ground. Huh, she thought, he's got a box just like Mike's, the one he keeps all the farm's money in. She'd only glimpsed it a couple of times. Mike kept it hidden away and this time of year it would probably be several thousand dollars. And when she saw that Darrell's box, which had spilled open with the pack, also had many rubber banded stacks of dirty bills, it was her turn to say, Shit. Darrell looked down at the money, I wish you hadn't a seen that, almost to himself. Before she could turn she was pushed to the ground, shoved facedown into the leaves and fir needles. He straddled her back and Amy tasted the musty dirt as she gasped and struggled, ending up on her back. She looked up and his eyes gave out a flat light, like two metal spoons. He wasn't much bigger but he had the leverage. She clawed a handful of dirt and threw. He cursed and reared back. She pushed him off and scrambled away. Cornered between the outcropping and the drop to the creek she tried to rush past him. He tackled her around the waist and threw her against the cart, spilling the wood. She rose up and he swung, spang! to the side of her head, sparks at the edge of her vision. He stood over her, panting. Hold still, he said. He looked down at her, then to the cliff. As he dragged her towards the edge Mike's voice came into her head, barking instructions. *Stand up! Focus! Do the work!* She kicked free and rolled to her feet while her mind cleared and her vision, like an aperture, twisted down to a circle, Darrell all she could see. He lunged and wrapped her up, dragging her back towards the edge. She twisted towards him and snapped a knee into the softness of his groin, a sickly groan as she pushed him away and listened to the voice, *Square Up!* Darrell came at her again. *Breathe into the punch*, as she threw a right; all the wood behind the arrow. She felt Darrell's nose flatten to his face, the gristle and cartilage moving and rearranging with the sound of a cleaver splitting a chicken. He dropped to his knees and swayed, a vacant grin on his face. Somewhere off to her right she thought she heard her name, a voice she remembered. But that must have been a different Amy because this Amy had a job to do. She reached down and scooped up a piece of sawn alder. Raising it like a rough bat, she squared her shoulders and swung. The wood whistled by her ear to a wet crunch. She felt his skull give way and heard his breath, pushed from his body as he hit the ground and tumbled off the edge, disappearing into the brush with a muffled clack of moss covered rocks at the bottom. And then she was being smothered, wrapped up from behind. Her calm broke and she was kicking screaming wailing; in her ear Mike's voice.

"Amy, Amy, its OK, its me," and the arms were his arms, arms she knew and she quit kicking and dropped the club. In a rush she came back into herself, blinking, gasping, sobbing and she was in the forest, the cart turned over, spilled wood, blood, her shirt torn. Mike's grasp was now a hug and she turned into his chest. She pushed Mike away, dropping to her knees, all fours, retching in the dirt. Mike rubbed her back while it all came up, finally, to dry heaves and sobbing. Amy shuddered and rolled to the ground.

Mike spoke, gently, "Let's get to the creek, the lower pool, and get you cleaned up."

He looked over the edge, "I'll check on Darrell," he said, though they both knew what he would find.

She washed the blood from her hands and arms, scooping the cold water to her face, the back of her neck. It hurt when she rolled her shoulders but she liked the feeling and her right hand stung from the water and the blood, her blood, ran from her knuckles, the sting like a badge, some kind of prize. Watching the drops from her face shimmer the water, she thought about what he had tired to do and what she had done and as the water calmed, it returned her gaze, level and calm. A few minutes later Mike returned and sat on the bank.

"Dumb luck," he said, "that I noticed the missing box," while she came over and slid next to him. He put his arm around her, "Not that you needed my help. I came running when your mom said you and Darrell were getting wood." He skipped a rock in the creek.

After that, the karmic balance at the farm wobbled. Candles and sage and crystals took up every surface in their cabin as her mother whispered Wiccan chants and incantations - when she was there. Mostly she left the cabin to Amy and it was Mike that came when the dreams struck. And while Darrell's death was ruled self defense the inquest drew attention to the farm it could have done without. So after Mike got hauled off on a cultivation charge and, in a Vodka induced confession, Amy's mother said she couldn't be in the 'same cosmic space as a killer,' Amy slung her pack over her shoulder and hitched into Eugene, then up I5 to Portland.

Amy started as someone, Sheila, touched her shoulder.

"Whoa, hon," Sheila said. "you OK? You look like you've seen a ghost," now laughing. "And you're up."

8

RACHEL DUG TO the bottom of her pack and pulled out her best jeans, best *fitting* jeans anyway, and a vintage rock and roll t-shirt along with a bit of make-up.

"Look at you. Where you going, Rach?," Brittany asked.

"Just on a little supply run," she replied. "I'll be back later tonight."

Properly attired, Rachel walked to the bus mall and boarded the 51, up Vista into the West Hills.

There was a deep red sky to the west and the lights of Portland were just coming up through the firs that ringed Council Crest Park. Josh stood on the curb sipping his beer on the warm June evening. The police would arrive around midnight to chase everyone home. But for now, skunk weed, cigarette smoke and hormones wafted from open car doors as Bastille, 21 Pilots and Taylor Swift made for a competing sound track. At his feet, lifted from his parent's garage, was a half rack of beer and a few of bottles of wine. They made him a popular guy and all was right with the world. In fact, strolling towards him, just beyond Tyler Wilson's pearl white BMW, was Rachel Barton, looking like someone who might want a beer. He didn't know her well - they'd had English and psych together but she'd transferred out late junior year - some kind of alternative high school he'd heard, or maybe rehab.

She gave Josh a quick smile and he reached into the box for a cold one. But as she walked by the beemer, Tyler pushed the passenger door open.

"Hey Rachel, what's going on?," he said.

She leaned into the car for moment, then slid in and shut the door. Damn, Josh got the cocaine part but didn't think she was a line and blow job kind of girl. And a blow job was definitely the going rate for any of Tyler's stash. Oh well. He drained his beer and reached for another one. But, as it turned out, she didn't know the going rate. The door flew open and Rachel was out on the pavement. She rolled to her feet and spat into the car.

"Wilson, you're an asshole."

"Fuck off," came the bored response.

She spun and stomped towards Josh.

"Give me one of those," she said. Ah, a damsel in distress. It was a beautiful evening after all. As he reached in his pocket for the opener she grabbed the bottle, wheeled and threw. There was loud pop and everyone was silent. The glass in the BMW's back window was spidered and covered in foam, brown glass tinkling to the pavement. The driver's door flew open, "What the fuck?" Josh, her knight, stepped in front. But before Tyler got two steps, Josh heard the sound of breaking glass and was hip-checked off the curb. She was breathing hard, holding the neck of a broken wine bottle. Her breasts strained the faded Depeche Mode t-shirt and Josh stared, stupefied. She looked back at Tyler.

"C'mon dick head, I'll cut your balls off."

From somewhere off to the right, "I wouldn't try her, Wilson, she'll fuck you up." The mood on the hill broke and everyone, including her and Tyler, started laughing. "OK, OK," his hands up. "But I'm sending you a bill for the window." She stared at Tyler with a crooked smile and ran the back of her wrist under her nose. "In your dreams," she replied. "Hey Josh," Tyler said, "the least you can do is throw me one of those beers." Josh tossed the beer to Tyler as the young woman pressed an unopened bottle towards him.

"Sorry," she said. "I owe you some beers. Josh, right?"

He popped the cap, foam spilling to the pavement as they clinked bottles.

9

SHE'D MANAGED TO extricate herself from Josh trading a made-up phone number for a bottle of wine. Too bad, he was a nice guy. But Rachel was quite sure that, if they knew where she was living, Josh's parents would not approve. She made another round on the hill, a few more touches, then quietly slipped out of the circle of light towards the trail. She dropped into the trees, using her phone for light. But she wouldn't need it much. She'd been exploring these trails since she was a kid. The firs enveloped her, opening for Greenway Street, then Fairmount Avenue, finally dropping into the wooded ravine that led to the city below. After a while the trail crossed Sherwood Drive, a quiet street lined with the old Portland homes of brokers, doctors and lawyers. The Connelly's house was just up the street. Mr. Connelly was her father's financial guy and she used to play here when she was little. Sure enough, both Mercedes were left open. A $10 latte stash in the ashtray of the blue one, and Mrs. Connelly's purse on the passenger seat of the black one. She'd had liked the family growing up, so she only took the cash, a couple hundred by the feel of it, and left the rest. Then she re-entered the dark woods and made her way down towards the city. When Rachel emerged from the forest, she stood under a secluded street light to survey her haul. A few beers, two bottles of wine and some weed, along with two wallets and a purse. Not bad, she thought, reshouldering her back. And there was one more thing, stuffed down a back pocket. Guys were so easy and when Tyler had the mirror out, really thought she was going to give him head, she'd palmed the vial. The broken window hadn't really been part of the plan although it did make for a nice diversion. But once he had his zipper down and his hand on the back of her neck, the memories flooded in and she'd sort of lost it.

She held the glass vial up to the light. At least a gram. She'd be a popular girl when she got back to camp.

10

JEFFREY'S ALARM WENT off at 5:25am. Not that he really needed it. There were things to do and one simply got up and did them. Across the bed, his wife Genny uttered the gentle if distressed snore of barbiturates, alcohol and the current anti-anxiety med. There's a bed size called a California King. Bigger than a regular King-sized bed; an expanse that allowed them to say they slept together. But only in that they occupied the same acreage, like two farmers sharing a pasture. They each had their own bathrooms and closets, each large enough for a small family. Sometimes they had sex, or he had sex with her. Short grunting episodes that might be called facilitated masturbation by him and a distasteful duty, at the very least, by her. But it allowed them to say, to think, that they were a 'happily married couple' because they did the things that such people did, or so they assumed. But, thankfully for Genny, it didn't happen too frequently as he had other outlets for his appetites which sometimes included mild bruising and a mollifying gift. And there was another outlet. One that seemed to exist outside the conscious mind of all involved, and was currently on the street.

As he did most every morning, Jeffrey went to the large window at the far end of the room and gazed over the city. Today was a low gray sky with a smudge of pink to the east, past the shrouded flanks of Mt Hood. His great grandfather had built this house early last century. He'd had the workmen erect a scaffolding, a rickety 75-feet high with a small platform at the top, facing east, where this window, the window Jeffrey gazed from would sit. And the workmen would see his great grandfather up there, arms crossed, looking out through a window in a house that didn't yet exist, on a city that didn't quite exist yet either.

Below to Jeffrey's left, down the bank that fell way from the house, stood a single Douglas fir maybe eighty feet tall. And while it was beginning to block the view, he would not allow the tree to be cut. It was thought to be some sort of memorial to his father, another Barton who had increased the family fortune in the harvesting, mowing really, this great tree of the northwest. Of course, growing a tree was nothing if not ironic as Jeffrey's father had cut down every old growth Douglas fir he could during the insane drunken swaggering 'cut anything that grows' days of the Reagan years. But that wasn't really it.

He had been five years old when one of his father's hunting dogs had found Jeffrey's new kitten and, shaking it like a rag doll, killed it. As Jeffrey sat distraught, the mangled kitten in his lap, his father approached, a stern, disappointed look on his face.

"Jesus Christ, Jeffrey," he'd said. "Pull your self together. Its only a cat so you can quit crying like a girl. Have the Terrence get rid of the thing."

When his father found out that the groundsman had helped Jeffrey hold a small service for the kitten, had planted a small fir tree on its grave, Terrence was fired and Jeffrey was told to never speak of it again. And so lessons were learned. Some in this very room. A few years later he had been exploring his parent's forbidden bedroom during a large and noisy party. He heard voices approaching, the small laughter of conspiracy. Young Jeffrey burrowed deep into the recesses of his mother's walk-in closet, scented with his mother's Chanel. Through the silken garments, he'd observed his father bed the mother of a friend. So a grown Jeffrey always looked in both closets.

But those thoughts passed lightly if at all this morning. With a last long view over the city, and decent chunk of the state, he turned from the window and began his day.

11

THE DREAM HAPPENED with a frequency, this dream anyway, sometimes years, sometimes months apart but never disappearing. And while the location varied it was generally the trailer Eldon grew up in or an unnamed camp or squad bivouac in Helmand province. On the surface, the place, the dream, the people, the circumstance held nothing to fear, not much out of place. In fact, everyone in the dream - his parents, grandmother, platoon brothers and sisters - seemed to be having a pretty good time. It was a party even. But Eldon would know better. The mood would be over saturated, like a Kodachrome photo or when you bite into a dessert that has too much sugar; cloying and bitter. The sense of foreboding would be overwhelming, without name or particulars but immense. He would go around the room, begging everyone, *Something really bad is going to happen.* We need to get out of here. *We need to leave now!,* he'd plead. And they'd ignore him, or laugh at him, Cmon, Eldon. Everything's fine. Relax, they'd say. And since it was the people he cared about most in the world, nearly all of them gathered here in one place whether it was a dusty camp in Iraq or packed into his family's trailer in the desert of eastern Oregon, he couldn't go by himself, he couldn't leave them to face what he alone knew was coming. Except he never knew what exactly it was. Only that it was horrible, terrifying; a malevolence that never appeared before Eldon woke with a start, tangled in sweat soaked sheets. Nothing to do but pull on the running shoes and head out the door. Today it was a flat, gray dawn, with rain coming. Yesterday's sun forgotten. The locals called it June-uary.

Eldon lived in North Portland. Square blocks of bungalows on 50 x 100 foot lots built in the first half of last century. When the swollen Columbia River had broke its dike and inundated the mostly black enclave of Vanport in 1948, the community of transplanted black southerners, many of them former WWII Kaiser shipyard workers were, through overt conspiracy of the city fathers, forced to relocate. Sort of like New Orleans' Ninth Ward and Katrina, but different. There weren't any cops on freeway overpasses with shotguns, just white realtors and bankers that wouldn't show any houses or write any loans outside of the city's North and Northeast neighborhoods. A passive-aggressive, Oregon style of apartheid called redlining. When he'd moved in ten years ago the neighborhood was largely black. It was the closest thing to his grandmother's old Memphis neighborhood he could find. But the anglo hipsters had rediscovered urban living. So while it wasn't exactly a conspiracy there was something strangely convenient about the black folks getting moved in and moved out based on the whims of white realtors. No need for white robes and burning crosses. Simple economics did the trick. White hipsters were willing to pay crazy amounts of money for rundown rental properties. Neighborhoods where you wouldn't go on a dare ten years ago now had pet yoga boutiques and goateed middle aged programmers on beach bikes.

After his run, Eldon spent some time weeding the garden. Another mediative task that kept a center within reach. As he brushed the dirt from his knees he heard his name.

"Morning, Eldon," came over the back fence. His neighbor Betty Washington was out in her own garden.

Betty was Black, getting to seventy and a retired Portland librarian. Now she spent most of her time helping out at her church, trying to keep it afloat, since many of the parishioners had been scattered to the suburbs by gentrification. That, and she did some work for Eldon. He called her his secret weapon and she'd say, Oh hush, Eldon, but she knew it was true because other times she'd give a quick nod and say, Damn straight, excuse my French.

12

SHE'D BEEN ONE of the first Black hires at the Multnomah County Library. She loved working the research desk because this was long before the internet and google and all of that and if you wanted to find out something, then the library was it - whether you wanted to know how many bushels of wheat were harvested in Kansas in 1968 or what year Jackie Robinson broke into the majors.

She was also there when the first computers showed up, big noisy scary things that no one understood and didn't want any part of but they didn't seem so scary to Betty so she'd look over the shoulder of the computer guys, always guys, but they didn't think much of it. And she'd ask questions and they'd humor her, or thought they were humoring her, because it started to make sense and soon Betty did understand what they were doing. She didn't know why herself, but she was drawn to the machines and the idea that there was some kind of magic happening in there. So she'd follow the techs around, ask innocuous questions and there were a couple of guys, not many but a couple, that picked up her signal, that she also could channel these strange devices and they'd point out things, leave extra manuals behind and maybe a set of tools. But most of them just thought she was an overly curious colored woman, so they mostly ignored her because what could a woman, let alone one of her kind, possibly understand about these things. But after while, it got so they didn't have to call the tech guys when the machines were acting up. They'd just call Betty and, as near as the other librarians could figure, she'd be in there performing a mystical rite because back then, the machines were as much mechanical as electronic with tape reels and punch cards and big removable disks the size of dorm fridges. The word slowly got out and other branches would call, Hey Betty, mind dropping by and looking at something? So she was there when the first PCs showed up, and then the internet. And she just kept soaking it up, moving with the technology. Eventually some of the local tech firms got wind of her power and tried to hire her away. It'll be great for our diversity score, she'd heard the middle-aged white men say, thinking she was out of earshot. But really, she liked the library and the pay wasn't bad and the pension wasn't either. She also liked being there for the neighborhood kids because the white librarians didn't take them seriously but Betty was there, helping with their research projects and college applications.

When Eldon first moved in she was pleasant, but she mostly ignored him. What would she want to talk about a with a big old white boy with a hint of Tennessee twang. But it was a twang that sparked an old memory so when she found out he was from Memphis, and knew some folks down there, well, that made him a little better. So they'd talk over the back fence, trade some neighborhood gossip and she couldn't really remember how they got on the subject of what he did and what she used to do but he'd asked her to look into a couple things, and could she take care of this and then she was his business manager of a sorts, since she did the books for her church. And secret weapon.

13

"HOLD ON," SHE said, "let me give this back to you," and handed him a manila folder over the fence. "Its all copied and on the server," she said. "I added some family history stuff, too. Let me know how Tony goes."

Back in his kitchen Eldon washed his hands in the kitchen sink and turned the front right burner to Medium under a small cast iron pan. Then, measuring water into the teapot, turned on a second burner. He took two eggs from the refrigerator along with a block of cheddar cheese and a bottle of hot sauce. While he waited for the pan to heat he scooped oily coffee beans, none of that trendy light roast shit popular with the hipsters, into a German hand grinder he'd gotten at an estate sale and turned the crank. When the handle spun free he tapped the contents into the French press. He then broke the eggs into a small bowl and pulled a whisk from among the kitchen utensils stored in an old Folger's can. It was sort of a tribute to his grandmother who drank gallons of the stuff. She would have laughed at the attention paid his morning cup. Adding a decent pinch of salt, he scrambled the eggs. He grated a handful of cheddar cheese on to the cutting board and returned the block to the refrigerator. Rinsing the whisk, he laid it in the bottom of the sink. After testing the heat of the pan, the drop of water sizzled but didn't pop, he poured in the eggs and, reaching back to the Folger's can for a spatula, gave them a little swirl. After the eggs set for a moment he added the cheese on the left side and flipped the right half over. As the coffee water began to boil he turned off both burners and slipped the omelette on to the plate. Sitting down with his coffee and eggs, he opened the folder, R. Barton on the tab. Quaint, this packet of paper. But then, if you really wanted to make sure something stayed private, it didn't go on what Betty called the interwebs. He finished reading, closed the folder and washed the breakfast dishes, setting them in the dish drainer. Finally, he wiped the last of the cheese and ground coffee from the counter and folded the dish towel onto the oven handle. It was eight AM. Just enough time for a shower and the drive downtown. He was meeting an old friend for coffee. Just before leaving the house, he made a call. It went straight to voice mail.

"Hey Tony, I'll see you at ten. But can you check and see if you've got a runaway report on a girl, Rachel Barton. I'm working for her dad. I know you can't tell me much. Just wondering if she's crossed the radar. Thanks."

He fired up the Impala, slipped Howlin' Wolf into the CD player, and headed downtown.

14

MEL, WHO LOOKED a bit like Burl Ives if he'd been on the street for fifteen years, used the one good leg to push himself up to his usual spot on the westside approach for the Hawthorne Bridge. A place where the lanes joined and the traffic slowed making it the perfect spot for a cherubic and bearded old man with one leg, like a padded tree stump, to extract pity and tribute. Mel carried a big smile. And, even though he'd left his faith far behind in Vietnam, he held a hand lettered sign that said *Disabled Vet. Anything helps. God bless.* And today should be a pretty good day. Tom McCall Waterfront Park was crowded with the carnival, music venues, beer garden - all the things that came with Rose Festival.

Most people thought he'd lost the leg in Vietnam and Mel didn't dissuade folks from seeing him as an injured war veteran. But that wasn't it, and it certainly didn't meet his PR vision. In another life, Mel could have been a marketing exec pulling two fifty a year. But one uses their gifts where they can. In his case, it was the street. Too much drinking, too much bad food, and feet that weren't dry from November until April. For a while, he'd balanced the pain with alcohol and whatever else he could find. But the pain became too much, the scale tipped and he passed out one rainy February Tuesday in Old Town in the middle of Third

55

St. When the CHIERS van showed up, the van gets them off the street and into the drunk tank - so they can sober up enough to repeat the cycle - they said, Hey, its that guy from Rudolph again, chuckling as they pulled on their latex gloves. And when they tried to get him up, get some words out of him, he just groaned and his shoe slipped off, well it wasn't really on anyway, just sort of pulled over the swollen club of his left foot. The stench, the smell of blood and puss and rotting flesh leaking through the six pairs of socks just about knocked them over. At the hospital the socks that had to be cut away from the foot but they needn't have gone to the trouble with the gangrene, the kind you see in tropical disease text books. So they went ahead and took it off just above the knee and here he sat with his sign and his smile and a kind word for everyone, tribute paid or not.

Mel heard his name and turned. A friend walked towards him with a smile and brown paper sack with spots of grease.

"Well there, stranger. How the hell are you Eldon?"

"I'm good, Mel. Just thought you might need some lunch. There's a couple of Little Big Burgers in there, bacon and blue cheese, if I remember right."

"Indeed it is, sir," Mel said. He took the bag and opened it, taking a big whiff.

"Thank you, Eldon. You are a gentleman and a scholar. To what do I owe this visit?"

"Well," Eldon said, "I'm wondering if you could do me a favor. I'm looking for a runaway and I'm thinking she might be on the waterfront. I'm also looking for a couple guys. Wondering if you can keep your eyes open."

"I can indeed," Mel said. He looked down to the esplanade below. The lunch time crowd of tourists, office workers and homeless sharing the day.

"Down there is young Curt. I believe you two are aquatinted," Mel said.

"We are," Eldon said. "But I'm afraid he's slipping away."

Curt walked the sidewalk below, clearly on his own frequency.

"He might be," Mel said. "But he could probably use a kind word."

Eldon gave Mel a few pictures and a burner phone.

"Just shoot me a line if you see anything," he said, passing him a twenty. "I'll go say hey to Curt."

15

MATT SAT AT his desk the next morning, still a little shaky from the alley, a hangover and something else. Maybe someone else. He stared out the window waiting for the aspirin to kick in and his stomach to calm from the food cart breakfast sandwich. The pain behind his eyes was taking its sweet time. He winced at the eastern sun, bright even through the fancy half-blind, and thought there were times that one of the interior offices where the interns and clericals sat didn't seem so bad. At least he didn't think he was going to have to return his breakfast the hard way. But it was still early. He fumbled around his office, trying to look busy. Somewhere between the coffee maker, the emails and the lease proposal he was supposed to be working on, he found himself on the Mary's Club website, the Dancers tab. There with Sheila and Viva was Amy. A few pictures, and message board - *Great show last night at Marys!* from someone tagged Lonesome Larry - and a calendar. *I'll be at Club Diamond this Thursday from Noon to 6pm. C'mon by!*

16

JEFFREY HAD LOOKED through Genny's phone, something he did often without her knowledge, and had easily discovered the affair. The emotion he felt was not jealousy or hurt. No, more like Jeffrey was pissed that someone was using something of his without his permission. That she didn't mean much to him was beside the point. This wasn't the first time and usually all it took was a threatening phone call to end it. But when he looked into the paramour's background, he thought Cory Stalmer might be someone useful. He had arranged a meeting and confronted him with the affair. Cory had snorted, What the fuck you gonna do? I'd say you got a lot more to lose than I do. And Jeffrey realized they had much in common. Useful indeed. Although there were times when Jeffrey wondered who was using whom.

<h1 style="text-align:center">17</h1>

TONY WAS ALWAYS late. Gotta case poppin', he'd say. So Eldon sat in a coffee joint near the downtown precinct, texting with Betty about another manila folder, something about a missing piece of jewelry from a Lake Oswego home with a limited number of suspects, all rich, and could he do some discrete enquires as they didn't want to involve the authorities, when Tony finally rolled in. Despite his bright friendly eyes and impish grin, Detective Tony Mason was not an overly enthusiastic social studies teacher, but a 20-year Portland Police veteran, homicide division.

"What do you mean she's not in your data base?," Eldon said. "Don't you keep a log of calls, runaways, that sort of thing? My client said he'd told the police but they weren't doing anything."

"Yeah, we keep track of those calls. And I checked. One thing he's right about. With all the calls we get, there's not much we can do, just don't have the resources unless we get something like a credible location, maybe imminent danger, something like that. But no, there's no record of a call from Jeffrey Barton, or anything coming up with Rachel Barton's name on it."

Eldon pulled out his phone and showed Tony a picture. "Know this guy?," he said.

"Gee, what happened to him, Eldon? Looks like a sleeping baby. Except for the swollen eye." Tony said, eyebrow raised with a half smile.

"Nothing, he was just taking a nap. Thought he looked peaceful. The license said Randy Weston. Ring any bells?"

"Yeah, I know the guy. Grew up in outer SE, small timer, drugs, maybe some weapons. What's up?"

"Not sure. He was in an alley with a knife and teenage girl before he got sleepy. Not his style then?"

"No, but it might have something to do with one of his buddies. Cory Stalmer. Frankly, I don't know why Cory puts up with the guy. He's kind of a fuck up but they go back to third grade or something. Now, Cory, that guy's a bad dude. Into a bunch of shit, but smart, has guys like Randy doing the scutwork. And teen aged girls are in there somewhere. You know who you should ask? Meghan. She worked a case of his once."

She was meeting Eldon at 2pm. He'd asked about someone she hadn't thought of, hadn't wanted to think of, for a very long while. In most of the cases she dealt with she was able to find some hint of humanity. And in many of them, once you gave them a voice, more humanity than anyone thought possible. And because of that, she rejected the term evil. In nearly all her cases the person in front of her was manufactured by their circumstances. That didn't mean they shouldn't be separated from society. But she wasn't sure the term evil fit. But every once in a while she had a case that made her question that assertion. None more than the folder she held in her hand.

* * *

Eldon left downtown, heading north up Hwy 30 past the oil tank farms and railroad tracks that hugged the river through industrial NW Portland. Hell in waiting, he thought, passing a crow washing itself in an oily puddle. When the big one came, the earthquake that hits the west coast every three or four hundred years, the soil, mostly fill dirt, would liquify and several million gallons of petroleum product would spill from the ruptured tanks. That black river would need to find just one arcing power line and they'd be able to see the glow from Seattle.

Crossing the high gothic arch of the St Johns Bridge his truck dropped into St Johns proper - probably the last neighborhood in Portland to resist gentrification but even here, slowly losing the battle. Meghan said she'd meet him at Marie's, a beautifully shabby joint on Lombard with shag carpet, pool tables and high-backed red velvet booths. His eyes adjusting to the dim, he spotted her at the bar. Looking like Amanda Plummer's less crazy sister, she sat stirring her coffee.

"Hey, Eldon."

"Hey, Meghan, how you been? Still hanging with the civic all stars?"

While she took other cases, Meghan had the unofficial title of death penalty investigator. It was her job, once a maximum sentence came down, to humanize the convicted. Perhaps enough to thwart the needle. The stories she heard of violence and depravation would keep most folks staring at the ceiling all night, their therapist on speed dial. He didn't know how she did it. She was the kindest person he knew. While Eldon recounted the alley he showed her the picture of Randy.

She shrugged. "Don't know him," she said.

He told her about Rachel and the alley, Matt and his client. And Cory.

"Tony said I ought to ask you about him," Eldon said. 'He thought Randy was probably working for him. You had his case once, right?"

Meghan always said she'd never worked a case where the convicted didn't undergo terrific trauma and privation. Cory wasn't any different.

Cory and his twin brother, she said, when they were about ten, got into their dad's drug money and spent it all on food. The dad had been on a three day bender. When he got home and saw the food wrappers and the soda cans and the empty stash he dragged them to the sink and hand cuffed them together to the drain pipe and left for another week. Somewhere around day three they threw a shoe through the front window while the mailman was making the delivery. Its weird what shit like that will do to people. Cory's brother runs a street ministry in St Louis, just got an award from the governor. But Cory went the other way, deep.

Meghan stared down into her coffee, moving the spoon in slow circles.

"So, he'd handcuffed this guy," she said, "one of his dealers, to metal desk at an empty warehouse off Highway 212. Maybe the guy had lost or spent or shot up the product or the money. Or maybe it was just for fun. The next day, when the realtor showed up to check the property, she thought the red swirls were a pattern in the linoleum. It finally dawned on her and she threw up her double latte in the parking lot while dialing 911. He'd dragged that desk around the room, trying to get away from the taser and whatever lawn and garden implement Cory'd brought with him. But he'd gotten sloppy, or too excited, and left some evidence. It looked like he was going down hard so the defense hired me, a head start on a bad outcome. But it didn't matter. Two sisters, meth heads from down the valley, swore he'd been with them all that night. Case over. Except, six months later, no one could find either of them."

"Nice guy," Eldon said. "So I need to get this girl off the street."

"Something like that," she said. "I gotta go, its my Head Start volunteer gig. Trying to catch them early, you know? Let me know how else I can help."

She headed towards the door, then stopped and turned.

"Hey, Eldon," she said.

"Yeah?"

"If you get in close with him, and the shit goes down."

"Uh huh."

"And its you or him, and you've got him square, but you stop because, well, you're Eldon?"

"Yeah?"

Meghan paused, considering her words, "Well, maybe don't."

18

"WHAT THE FUCK? You lost her?," Cory said, shoving Randy hard against the wall, a forearm under his chin. But Randy just waited, relaxed. They'd known each other a long time and this was just how Cory said hello. Well, how he said hello if you had bad news for him. If he was truly angry Randy would be bleeding on the floor, or worse. Thankfully, he'd only seen it done, and had to clean up the mess. And he wasn't sure what it was about this particular little piece of ass, why Cory wanted this one, but he knew better than to ask. When Cory got something in his head, you just went with it. She did have a rocking body, but there were so many others. Whatever. He usually got his turn after Cory was done anyway. Randy massaged his throat and told Cory about the alley.

"Jesus Christ, Randy, I just asked you to grab one little girl and you fuck it up. And you get your ass kicked by some cowboy. I swear to god, if we didn't go back, I'd kill your sorry ass."

"Fuck, Cory," Randy said, "What was I supposed to do? It was some weird shit, I'm telling you. Its just me and the girl in the alley, its all going down nice and easy then this dumb fuck shows up out of nowhere. That was going to be easy enough to deal with but then John Wayne rides up. Big guy, too. Knew what he was doing. I'm not that easy, Cory. You know that."

"Yeah, I guess you're right," Cory said. "Let's not do that again, OK? Any sign of her since?"

"Naw," Randy said, "but I figure she must still be around the waterfront with the carnival and sailors and the crowds. Too much easy money, food, drugs, whatever. I'll find her. I got enough people looking."

"Fuck yeah, you're going to find her. Anyway, enough of that shit. How's recruitment going anyway? The fleet's in town, dude."

Recruitment was another word for managing but the actual word was pimping. Prostitutes and strippers constituted another one of Cory's many lines of business. His business model, and he had one, was anything that polite society considered morally repugnant even if they were more about choices made by adults, namely drugs and sex. Oh sure, Cory was into the truly morally awful stuff as well. Rather enjoyed it, in fact. But there was real money to made with the fact that this country was founded by stick-up-the-ass Puritans. Frankly, this whole legal cannabis thing kind of pissed him off. But for now, shipping Oregon's righteous bud to states where it wasn't legal yet was working out pretty well. And really, it didn't matter, There would always be things that people would pay for.

19

MATT MADE IT through lunch without hurling. But couldn't see himself getting through the afternoon without a nap or some other diversion. So he mumbled something about a property visit to the front desk and took the elevator to the garage. Matt's job involved a lot of local windshield time with site visits, working with contractors, architects and building engineers, checking on his tenants. Usually these sites were new Class A buildings downtown or trendy rehabs in some recently gentrified neighborhood. But today's site visit was a nowhere near downtown and it might be a while before this neighborhood saw many hipsters.

He was on some sort of rail, like he was watching himself get in his car and head east. He crossed the river on Burnside Street and drove through toney Laurelhurst to 82nd Ave where he turned south and entered an unending landscape of grubby strip malls, used car dealers and adult video stores. There was another turn east, out Foster Road, finally ending in the rutted parking lot for Club Diamond. Reaching under the seat, he retrieved an old Portland Timbers cap and pulled it low. As if anyone he knew would be out here on a Wednesday afternoon. But then he might have been hiding from himself a little, too. Without thinking much about it because otherwise he'd smack himself in the side of the head and roll back to the office, he pulled open the door. His eyes adjusted and there was Amy at the bar, with that notebook again. What the hell was she doing with that thing anyway, he thought.

"Hey, Amy," he said. "Its Matt, from yesterday," sounding like the dork in some high school comedy.

But she could see what kind of shape he was in so she let it go and smiled.

"Hey, Matt," she said. "Looks like you kept going last night. You OK?"

She was pretty good at picking up the creepy stalker vibe and he wasn't giving that one off but he was giving off the confused married guy vibe and she knew how to handle that one as well. Plus bonus points for the hangover. Usually, they just needed a little friendly conversation and maybe a dance or two and they wandered home. Maybe no less confused but at least with some pleasant conversation and mental images that would come in handy later.

"You don't look so good," she said. "I'm up if you want to join me. I've been working up some new pole moves."

And this time he did join the other silent men at the rack, with a soda water and lime. He sipped the water and tried to figure out how to look at her. He really did want to look but he also kind of liked her and was it OK to stare at a woman like that? But then she was a stripper and this was her job and she was pretty good at it. So finally he just sat back and put down his bills like the rest of the guys. A bit more than the rest of the guys actually since she had kind of rescued him the other day.

Three songs later they were back at the bar. They tried to resume the music thread but that didn't seem to be going anywhere so he asked her about the notebook.

"I was going to say you were a writer or something," he said, "but it looks like something else."

He knew it wasn't any of his business but he was having trouble with the filter today. But she didn't seem to mind. In fact, she brightened.

"Oh yeah, that's my rental notebook. I've got a three houses so far, and looking to pick up a couple more. I make some money, buy some paint or light fixtures. Plus I need to keep track of the contractors."

She tipped her head towards the rack.

"Can't do this shit forever," she said.

"So, no offense," he said. "But how'd you get into this?"

"You mean, How'd a stripper get into real estate?," she said.

"Well, um."

"Just giving you shit," she said, bumping shoulders.

"It was a customer actually," she said. "One of my regulars was a retired real estate guy. I got the sense he'd done pretty well. But he'd come in and we'd get to talking and I asked him what he did and I said I always wanted to get into that, you know, passive income and everything. And he said it wasn't that hard, do the homework, start with one or two properties and go from there. He asked me if I had any money saved and I had some, not too much, and he ask me how much. So I told him and he was in a week later with a listing to show me. Two weeks later I closed on the place, totally freaked out of course. But I got some renters and started doing some improvements. And he'd come in with another listing but pretty soon I could pick out my own places and so that's how it went."

So now it was the blues and real estate and he was in commercial real estate and she had residential property but there were the same problems with tenants and renters and contractors and bankers.

"So, Matt," she said, my turn. "None of my damn business but you look like one confused boy. You doing all right?"

And Amy morphed from dancer to real estate tycoon to therapist and the next twenty minutes was Amy nodding, and uh-uhing, and what else would he talk about except his wife, the marriage, the miscarriages and everything else.

"Ah jeez," he said, "you don't need to hear this shit."

But he knew he needed to tell it and she let him.

"Listen Matt," she said. "Sounds like you got a pretty good thing there. So yeah, stop by anytime, we can talk about music or real estate or whatever. But you seem like a nice guy with a pretty good situation. Its my professional advice to not fuck that up. Now get out of here. I'm up."

20

THE ALARM BLARED on the bedside table. Amy groaned, pushed off covers and swung her feet to the floor. Oh man, she said out loud, that was a long shift. She pushed her fists into the small of her back and yawned. The night's tips had been pretty solid - enough to cover today's drywall and labor, for sure. But damn, home at two-thirty and she needed to get the crew going by seven-thirty in the fucking AM. She did some stretching to get the kinks out, pulled on her Carhartt's and headed out the door to her truck. Just enough time to hit Mr Plywood for supplies, where she'd grab some not really very good coffee and a donut from the box they kept by the contractor entrance. She didn't make a habit of it but desperate times and all that. She wanted the house rented out by the end of the month. The place was a pretty sorry sight; a refurb drug house she got off foreclosure. And it was built in the seventies, the low point for both building codes and anything resembling a soul. Amy damn sure planned to make some money from her houses. That was the whole point. But she also knew it would be a home for someone so she'd put in a few extra touches. She'd also get the furnace and insulation up to spec, maybe some double pane windows, too, so it wouldn't cost too much to live in. Plus, she pretty much rented to single moms or families. They were generally good for the rent.

Pulling up to the curb in front of the house she could see the crew in the front room, the walls open to the studs. Drinking their coffee and wolfing their gas station burritos, smoking their cigarettes and nursing their hangovers and generally getting ready for the day. Hanging and sanding drywall was about the most miserable work on any job. Consequently, the crews were made up of various dead-enders, ex-cons, alkies and the like. Walking in the front door, a 5-gallon bucket of mud in one hand, a box of dry wall screws under the other she recognized one of the crew, a new guy, Juan, Julios's brother or something and fresh out of the joint, from the club last night. He must have thought she was delivery girl or something. If he'd known who she was he might have kept his thoughts to himself.

"Hey there little momma," he said. "Saw you last night. That's a sweet little ass you got there. Maybe you show me sometime, just you and me. Maybe I can get some of that ass in the back room."

She glanced at Julio, her crew lead, with a look that said, Are you kidding me, and he looked back with a combination of horror and apology.

"Whoa there, Juan," he said, "take it easy, man."

"Its cool, Julio, I know how this delivery girl spends her evenings. I figure she might like to make little on the side," he said, grabbing his crotch.

Clearly, Julio hadn't mentioned the boss. The boss being Amy. So, just like that, she picked up a short length of two by four and pinned the smirking punk to the wall at his neck. His face went red, then purple and she grabbed him by the collar, throwing him to the ground.

"Listen, you little fuck, you talk about what you want somewhere else. But you do not disrespect me on my job site, not when I'm signing the checks."

She pulled out her wallet and dribbled a few $20s on his gasping form. Then prodding his kidneys with the piece of lumber, she said, "That should cover you for the week. You've got two minutes to get your shit and get off the property."

Amy looked over to Julio.

"Listen, bro. No more assholes, OK?"

"Yes, ma'am."

"Alright gentlemen, let's get to work. Looks like we're a little short handed today."

21

ONCE AMY GOT the crew sorted out she climbed in the pick-up and headed back home. She reached under the bed and pulled out a small wooden box. She knew better than to leave the box under her bed. But between club shifts and running her contractors the days and nights and tips got away from her. After a week it might be a couple thousand dollars, or more. She organized the stash, put it into the bottom of her canvas tool bag and headed out to her bank in the suburbs. There were closer banks but she didn't want to be seen with that much cash in her own neighborhood. And maybe one more thing. It's not that she was ashamed about being a dancer. She wasn't. But she didn't like the looks and the attitude she got outside the club. She liked to keep things in compartments. But there were times when she had to be in the real world as a dancer and it bugged her. Going to the bank, for example, with the smirks and side glances. It was the condescension that pissed her off. The doughy bank staff might have their ill-fitting clothes on. But they seemed pretty trapped and mildly pissed off at that. Amy had a following and good rep and if she was in a shitty club, she moved on. Plus, she had a plan. Today's stack was going to finish that bathroom. She probably made more than the poly-cotton dress shirt and panty hose crowd anyway. Hell, she bet they didn't have health insurance either. So yeah, they could just go fuck themselves. Except for Connie.

Amy and Connie had developed an odd acquaintance over the last few months. For Amy, it had something to do with not getting the judgment hit when she pulled the bills out. And she thought Connie got some kind of thrill out of their chats. *A real stripper.* So Amy would make the trip out to Beaverton, and there would be Connie, plump and fifty-ish, third station from the left. She'd light up when Amy pushed her way through the door, the whoosh of traffic from Canyon Road entering with her, the work coat decorated in dry wall dust and paint. If there was a line, Amy would let people go ahead, waiting for Connie's station to clear.

"Afternoon, Amy," she said. "Always good to see you. How are you today?"

"Just fine, Connie. You?"

"You know, I'm OK", she said, which came out as *I'm bored*, and they'd catch up on Connie's kids and Amy's latest project. They didn't talk about her night job so much.

Amy pulled the bills out of the tool bag and put them on the counter. Neatly stacked and sorted, left to right, ones, fives, tens and some twenties. Once in while, maybe after a bachelor party, there might be a fifty or a hundred dollar bill.

"Hmmm, business good then?"

Amy laughed, "Yeah, not bad."

It was as close as they'd come to discussing the source of Amy's deposits.

When the transaction was complete and the money put away, Amy would ask for a couple hundred back - fives, tens and twenties. For Amy, it was superstition, a sort of psychic money laundering. And there may have been something to that. But really, it was more about the compartments, keeping things separate. Plus these bills didn't smell like stale beer. Mostly she talked about the latest house project and today's morning encounter.

"Oh!," Connie said with a hand to her mouth. "None of my business, dear, but you are being careful."

"Yes, Connie. I'm being careful. How's Bob?"

"Just fine, dear."

Connie glanced at her watch as she snapped the bills in counting.

"About now," Connie said, "he's probably counting the minutes until the 4:37 bus and wondering what I'm making for dinner tonight. Yep, pretty exciting life I've got."

Amy knew that Connie had been married to Bob, a county employee, for 35 years and they had a couple of grown kids with grandkids on the way. Sometimes Amy envied her organized life, quiet and predictable, with meat loaf and 60 Minutes on Sunday evening. But not for very long.

Connie swore it would be the next time, the next time Amy came in. She'd ask her if she wanted to get a glass of wine, ask her about her crazy life, and just maybe, bring up a thing or two of her own. The young woman was about her daughter's age, but Connie and her daughter didn't get along so well. Plus she wanted to talk about things she'd never discuss with her daughter, or anyone else she knew, for that matter.

As she counted the bills, she looked to her left, opposite a small collection family photos. Along with the stapler, paper clip dispenser and scotch tape, there was a greeting card with a picture of the Space Needle on the front. The kind you might get in a hotel gift shop. Inside was a brief note, 'A pleasure to meet you. All the best. Regards, D.' Dan was from Spokane.

They'd met a few months ago at the Seattle Hyatt, each in town for a regional training. Sitting next to each other in the windowless conference room she thought he had a cute smile as they shook hands. His hand felt nice in hers. She'd worn her "fancy work dress." Professional, to be sure, but it showed just a bit of cleavage and during the day, she'd catch Dan looking at her breasts and it was something she didn't mind. When they got partnered off on a ridiculous team building exercise, they'd both decided that the trainer was an idiot, and that led to a day of shared jokes and a couple of drinks at happy hour and dinner where they'd laughed like old friends, or something else. She didn't really remember a conversation about it or an invitation. They had paid for dinner, separately, of course, they needed to file expense reports after all, and simply gone up to his room. As they reached his door, Connie, heart pounding, extended her hand. Thanks for a very nice evening, she said, then turned and walked away. Regretting it even as she made her way down the hall, she went back to her room, took a bath and went to bed.

Ever since, she'd thought about how it might have gone. Fumbling around like teenagers, apologizing and laughing, each electric from the feel of a strange new body, how the parts fit well if different, the exquisite knowledge that this was wrong and parting with a kiss before dawn because waking up together seemed like too much, that what they wanted had already happened. How she might have seen the night as a gift, an island of not, for once, doing what she was supposed to do. Instead, all she had was this card. She'd meant to respond, had even written one or two notes, never sent. And then time slipped away.

Connie printed the deposit slip and handed it to Amy.

"Always good to see you, dear," Connie said.

"You too, Connie. But I gotta scoot. I need to be somewhere at noon."

Yes, Connie thought, next time she'd ask Amy if they could meet up for a glass of wine. Bob could just get his own damn dinner.

22

CORY SAT AT a big table in the basement, scales and baggies, weed and meth and coke and whatever else he thought he could move strewn around him. He lit a few candles, took a little snort himself and cranked up Black Dalia Murder. A little death metal just the thing when you had to get shit done. At the moment meth, heroin and fentanyl were the big sellers. The meth went to the homeless population. It wasn't for fun, it was for safety. It kept them up at night so they could watch out for their stuff, and for the women, their own bodies. Collections could be a problem but he mostly let Randy and the next tier down worry about that. They knew all too well to make sure Cory got his money. Of course, the guys upstream from him had even less patience.

For the opiate customers he always said a little word of thanks to Big Pharma. They spent billions marketing the pill form, addicting many thousands, and creating a whole new batch of customers for the Cory's of the world. It used to be that guys like him would have to give a few bags away, create the demand. *The first one's free!* Now they came to him begging, thanks to the efforts of fresh-faced college graduates. The ex-sorority girls did especially well with the male doctors. All expense paid trips to Hawaii didn't hurt either. It was all on the up and up, nobody was getting blow jobs in the back office. But when a beautiful young woman asks a middle aged man to do something, in this case prescribe the latest miracle drug for the alleviation for pain, well, you moved a shit ton of pills. So yeah, business was good for Cory. And he'd started to add a little bonus to his deliveries. Naloxone, with the brand name Narcan, was the newest miracle drug from the industry. A nasal spray that would literally bring ODs back from the dead, or damn close to it. It turns out that too many dead customers were bad for business. It cut into his cash flow plus law enforcement would get interested. A few dead junkies were a tragedy but nothing polite society worried too much about. Weren't there always some? But too many became a problem, especially if there were too many white, middle-class deaths. But that's how the white power structure worked. The crack epidemic of the 90's preyed mostly on communities of color, especially the black community. That made it a crime problem. Even the Clintons used the term "super predator," conjuring images of hulking, chiseled black men, fueled by cocaine, in search of white women. Not all that far from Jim Crow, really. But now that the opioid crisis was killing whites, a staggering number actually, well, now we had a public health crisis on our hands. So while dead customers were generally bad, it turned out that *almost* dead customers were great for business. Since the goal of a lot of the junkies was to fly as close to the sun as possible, the idea that you could get just this close and pull the ripcord, well that really kept them coming back. And it was cheap, too. Now that he had a knock off Chinese supplier, it was the greatest marketing promotion he'd ever run. Cory zipped up the duffel and climbed the stairs.

He was loading today's deliveries in the cutout compartment in his trunk when his phone buzzed.

any progress?

Christ, Cory thought as he turned the key. Some people have no patience.

working on it. don't worry, I'll find her.

23

BETWEEN MEMPHIS AND where Eldon sat this morning, between then and now, the places and times and wanderings of a young man included a stint in the Army because that's what young men of limited means from the South did. His service included a couple of tours in Iraq which had IEDs and flaming Hummers and buddies dead in front of him but nothing out of the ordinary. And certainly far, far less than many he knew, many who wished they had bought it then and there. The watching, the witnessing and having to go on somehow seemed worse than being one of the honored dead. Others merely began the process there, in some back alley in Fallujah, the slow motion death. Some died there, others a week later, succumbing to their wounds, as the saying went. But for others the final part of the dying didn't happen until they got home, tried to make some sense of it and finally, unable to, finished the job by their own hand. Eldon had seen some, been through some but not so much that he thought it found any purchase, but of course it did and it would grow, like a weed, pushing up through the floor boards, a mutated and twisted thing. And while it would never die, was rooted too deep, you could cut it back, keep it low enough that you could get through the days and, what really mattered, the nights and look just like everyone else on the outside and even feel like anyone else, or what you imagined everyone else felt like, some of the time. But that didn't come without effort or attention. So Eldon and a dozen others sat in a mental health services waiting room at the VA hospital. He thumbed through a beat-up gossip rag. Old news about people he didn't care about. No World War Two vets here; Korean War either. Most of them were too old and they wouldn't be caught dead near the psych ward anyway. Too touchy feely. So the grizzled Vietnam vets sat along side their younger but more tightly wound Iraq and Afghanistan brothers. Mostly they ignored each other, part of them ashamed they were here, another part glad there was some kind of lifeline. Otherwise they might well eat a bullet. Enough of their friends already had. Here they were, with the thousand yard stare. Some of them with wives and girlfriends. All of them trying to pretend they weren't.

Eldon heard a mechanical click, the sound of unobtrusive but robust security, and a door opened at the far end of the room. Eldon's shrink Jay stuck his head out.

"Hey, Eldon. C'mon back."

The door closed with the same click. Keeping people in or out, Eldon wondered. Probably both.

Jay's office was small but the view over the city helped.

"So, how you been?," Jay asked. "Its been what, a couple of months?"

"Something like that," Eldon said. "But yeah, I'm OK."

Eldon always had mixed feeling about coming here. Most military guys did. *Embrace the suck* was the term of art. Meaning just handle it. And if you can't handle it, you must be some kind of fucking pussy. All that's all fine until you're having waking dreams with mangled body parts or crawling under the bed when a truck backfires. Eldon had seen his share of head Docs. Most of them sucked. But, there were a couple that had helped, Jay being one. So, here he was.

"What about you?," Eldon said.

"Oh, you know," Jay replied," too many patients. Budget cuts, blah, blah. What's been going on?"

"The usual shit," Eldon said. "Affairs, the gray haired controller swipes a hundred K from the place they've worked since high school, stuff like that."

Jay nodded and murmured, the way therapists do when they are listening or maybe composing their shopping list.

"Well, there is one," Eldon said. "I'm working on a case for a downtown lawyer. Looking for his runaway daughter. He's a bit of an asshole. Makes me wonder why she ran away. But still, the street's nowhere for a 17 year old girl. Fairly sure she's downtown. But she's laying pretty low. Thought I saw her a couple of days ago but I had to stop a guy from getting stabbed."

"Really?," Jay said, "my job is so boring."

"Some punk had pushed her into an alley, had a knife out. This guy stepped in. Pretty brave really, or stupid. He obviously didn't plan an exit strategy and the punk came after him with the knife. The girl ran off but I'm pretty sure it was her. And he knows her. Since she was a kid. Damned if he was going to admit to me though."

"So, what happened?"

"Well, let's just say I intervened. The gentleman with the knife will have a headache for a couple of days. But the guy was pretty shaken up and I let him buy me a beer. Frankly, I thought he might shed some light on the girl. He's a downtown office guy, out on his lunch hour. Actually, it turns out he's not as boring as he looks. Loves the blues, sounds like he plays some harp. Maybe we'll jam sometime."

"And maybe learn more about the girl," Jay said.

"Yeah, I guess. But he seemed like a decent guy and I could use someone to play music with. And unlike some of the runaway spouse cases I get, I think getting that girl off the street is probably a good thing. But its a funny one. The father definitely has an attitude, like the world belongs to him. I did some research on him and I guess it does."

"What do you mean?"

"He's a senior partner in one of the big downtown law firms, founded by his grandfather. That kind of shit. The family's fifth generation Oregonian. Which, around here counts for a lot."

Jay laughed. "Big fucking deal," he said. "I'm from New Orleans. There are prostitutes there that go back ten."

"Anyway, it would appear that the guy's pretty sharp in his own right. Doesn't want anyone to forget it though. Lots of pictures with senators and the like in his office. Wife seems to be the usual society type - charity boards, the right club memberships, home in the West Hills."

"But the guy gives you the willies?"

"Let's just say I know an asshole when I see one," Eldon replied.

Jay leaned forward. Enough of the small talk, he said. "How are the dreams?"

Eldon looked out the window. The lines tightened around his eyes.

A half hour and a hundred years later Eldon looked up, almost like waking. Jay looked at his watch. "Hey, Eldon," he said, "we should go. Its group time."

Many of the same guys from the waiting room, maybe twenty of them, pushed hard metal chairs into a circle. Jay gave his usual opening.

"This room is about respect," he said. "And telling your truth. And listening."

And so they began. First chatter, flicking shit, loosening up, trying to get to the place where they could talk and listen. As they got closer to the reason they came there was a change in the air, one they could almost touch. A realignment, like a door opening, and a guy spoke up, skinny with a haircut high and tight and full tat sleeves up his arms.

"OK, we were on this patrol in this tight little neighborhood in Baghdad," he said, the story unspooling. The guys listened, some looking at him, others staring at the floor or into space, that thousand yard stare. After twenty minutes, some hugs and fist bumps, the room was quiet again. Eldon's palms were damp and his breath was shallow but not that anyone could notice. Then someone else cleared his throat. It was Mel. He'd been here many times but had never spoken. So everyone fell silent.

"C'mon, Mel," someone called out.

Mel sat, quiet.

"Well, fuck," he said. "I guess this is for Frank."

He stopped, staring at his hands.

"Its cool, man," Eldon said. "Keep going."

Mel looked up and began again.

"So we're on patrol, somewhere out of Hue, and I'm on point," he said. "And Frank, who's barely shaving, is behind me and we're just joking around, why he didn't drink, why he didn't go chasing those little gook whores."

Mel paused.

"OK, sorry, that's not right," he said. "That's what we called them but that's not right. Shit, they were just little girls, too. Fucking hell, we were all kids out there. The goddamn grown ups were back at the DHQ, drinking in some bar in Saigon, or Honolulu or fucking DC. But the rest of us, Charlie, the girls, us poor grunts, we were all just a bunch of kids doing what the fucking grown ups said, and you want to know the honest truth, I never thought of that until just now, we were all just a bunch of goddamn kids. Anyway, how the hell I missed the wire I'll never know, walked right over it. But Frank caught it and I got blown to the ground, the wind knocked out of me and there's the ringing in my ears but not a scratch on me. But Frank's lying there, alive, but the lower half of his body is just blown apart. He started to go into shock but the medic was with the other platoon across the paddy, so Frank's just laying there, but there wasn't much we could do. We tried but there wasn't anything to grab on to, nothing to tourniquet so after a while he was just gone. So we picked up all the pieces of him we could find and bagged him and waited for the chopper and it took a while and we're all sitting there with Frank and nothing much to say and finally the chopper takes him away but there's no room for the rest of us and we have to walk back and now its starting to get dark and we knew it was some bad shit to be outside the wire at dark. But we got back without anything happening and made it back to our squad area. I sat on my bunk for a minute, just vibrating with Frank and being scared shitless being outside the wire and I just dropped my pack and helmet in front of my cot and, with Frank's blood speckled on my fatigues, walked down to Tyrone's bivi. I pulled out my money and Tyrone said, Shit Mel, heard about Frank, this one's on me, and here's a new rig too, and I sat down with Tyrone and the rest of them and they had to show me how to use it, how to get the right amount in the rig and there just wasn't going to be goddamn thing stopping me, and pushed that shit in and it all went away, 'Nam, Frank, all of it - and that was it. I was done, I was hooked right there. But when I came home, and got the job at the hardware store, got the wife, the kids and all that, I managed to stay clean. And I hung on as long as I could. But the little demons came back, knocked the ladder out from under me in the stock room, and fucked up my back. And this was fifteen years ago, you know, before they realized this opiate shit was bad for you and the doctor gave me a full bottle leaving the hospital and just kept em coming and then I was back where I was in that bunker with Tyrone again. Then shit started peeling off. The wife, the kids, the house - just sort of drifted away."

Mel looked up.

"So," he said, "I guess that's it. Thanks for listening."

First there was silence, each reliving their own versions. Then, Thanks for sharing, Mel, and, Oh man, that's rough, and a couple of hugs and they moved to the next guy, another story.

Later, as the session broke up, Eldon threw a chin at Mel.

"Hey, need a ride downtown?"

"Yeah, Eldon, That'd be great."

Out in the parking lot Mel hopped over to the Impala's front passenger seat while Eldon stowed the wheelchair in the trunk. Then Eldon fired up the 327, slipped in an Allman Brothers CD, and moved the shifter to D.

Eldon was a buddhist smoker. That is, he only smoked when the opportunity presented itself, or required it. He figured Mel would need a smoke and but there was something else. Jay, the dreams, the session, whatever - and something had gotten a little loose in his head, like a bowling ball in the trunk of a car. He needed that smoke, too.

"Hey Mel, pull that pack of Camels out of the glove compartment, would you."

Eldon reached down, pushing the cigarette lighter.

"Grab one for yourself. Don't suppose you've seen any sign of the girl, or those two guys?"

Mel tapped out a smoke and handed the pack across the seat.

"Can't say that I have," Mel said. Eldon took the pack, a slight tremble to his hand and Mel said, "You OK there, friend?"

"Yeah, I'm alright," Eldon said. "You know, session."

As if that explained it.

"I hear you, man," Mel said.

24

AFTER HE DROPPED Mel, Eldon headed across town. His other therapist was working the afternoon shift at a club in Northeast.

"Hey, E," Amy said, joining him at the bar. "What's up?"

"Oh. Nothing," he said. "Just needed a friendly ear."

Eldon got himself a beer and they talked some, more than some, about Mel and Iraq and the girl on the street. Jesus Christ, she thought, between Matt and Eldon and half her regulars did she need to be everyone's mom. Matt, all balled up with middle class angst, and upper middle class angst at that, like he can't decide whether to vacation in Hawaii or Mexico and its just killing him. And Eldon had different baggage but the manly man shit got pretty old too. Maybe not the strong silent type as much as the strong fucked up type. At least he's got a counselor now. A real one. But it seems like he's opened up some boxes he wanted closed. But do they really stay closed, she thought. Maybe not so often as before, but hers, the box with Darrell in it, it didn't really stay closed either. The shit crawls out and you don't know what to do with it, dead buddies and dying mothers and a runaway with her own box she's trying to keep closed.

"Hey there," Amy said. "You OK?"

"Yeah, I'm alright," he said. "But I was thinking it might be time to go see your mom. Get a little adjustment."

Amy's phone buzzed. She looked down and laughed.

"OK," she said, "that's weird. Its my mom."

But then her mom was kind of like that and Amy looked up at Eldon with a half smile.

"Hold on, mom," she said. "Its too loud in here," as she made her way to the door.

25

AFTER AMY LEFT the Coast Range and a portion of time had passed, her mom grew up some and maybe didn't smoke quite as much weed, and they found their way back to each other. Now Amy's mom, Jadie, on account of her green eyes, lived out on Sauvie Island, where two wide rivers met north of town. Maybe forty square miles of farms and hay fields on the south end and a wildlife refuge to the north with stands of alder and cottonwood, blackberry thickets and meandering sloughs with great rafts of geese and ducks, and herons and eagles. Jadie lived on the seam, between the two. You got to her place down a narrow dirt track, rattling across a wooden bridge over a muddy slough, to a clearing with the house on the edge of a field, maybe fifty acres.

Amy's mom was from LA, up one of the canyons in the Hollywood Hills with the movie stars and the pornographers and the drug dealers. Not the Valley, and not Orange County, home of Disneyland; a suburban wasteland Los Angelenos refer to as Beyond the Orange Curtain. You weren't a real Londoner unless you were born within earshot of Big Ben. Amy's mom would say it didn't matter how vague, through the smog, past the palm trees and SUVs and the billboards and strip mall signs for Thai restaurants and nail salons that you weren't from LA unless you grew up in sight of the Hollywood sign.

Even before the real estate developer built the sign to sell houses, *Hollywoodland* until the *land* fell down, the motion picture business made its way to Los Angeles. Because what the early cameras needed was light. A lot of light. And they also needed space. Enough space to build Babylon or New York or any town USA. And so the light and the space drew the studios and the studios drew something else. Amy had a theory about her mom and a certain strain of the LA blood line. Besides the light and the space the movies also needed people. Beautiful people. People that other people wanted to look at, to watch on the flickering screen. And so those people came to LA and when they weren't trying to get a part or waiting tables or taking a lunch meeting they did other things. Like breed. And they bred truly beautiful children. It also attracted all the things that come to money and fame and beauty and power, the things around the edges and Jadie knew about those, too. So Amy's mom, and Amy after, were a product of that place and time.

Amy plopped in the stool next to Eldon.

"Mom says you should head out tonight," Amy said. "I guess there are no major celebrity crises at the moment. She'd love to see you. Oh, she says to bring tacos from the mercado in St Johns; carnitas and chorizo."

Like many New Age practitioners, Jadie knew her way around a dollar bill and charged ten grand per day. Cash. But with a sixty city tour, or a movie with a budget nearing that of a federal agency hanging in the balance, the price wasn't an issue for her usual visitors. A corporate jet would drop into Portland Intl. and taxi to the private terminal. Eldon or sometimes Amy would be out front in a rented, late model SUV, preferably with tinted windows. Or sometimes it would be the Impala. The rock stars loved the Impala, Eldon and a lithesome Amy in the front seat, its engine rumbling to life, an old blues tune in the background like, well, something out of a movie. They'd make their way through town towards the island, dropping the entourage at a downtown hotel where they could get to Powell's Books or Voodoo Donuts because Amy's mom insisted that only the single traveler be allowed on the island. Eldon and the passenger would cross the bridge over the muddy water pulling up in front of the old farm house where Amy's mom, mid-fifties looking more like mid-thirties would be waiting on the porch. Like Stevie Nicks in canvas, khaki and farm boots, an aging rocker once told her. After Eldon rolled back towards town Jadie and her guest, her charge, would catch up and she might give them a hand-thrown mug of something, who knows what. But she's enough of a marketer to throw in some actual dirt so it always tasted like dirt but could be a hit of acid and a bit of mushrooms or it could be some ground up Dilaudid in an IPA because all they needed sometimes was a break and rest and good night's sleep or two. Or it could be some green tea and a long conversation with someone who didn't give a shit about who they were. They like the people that treat them likes stars but *love* those who don't, Jadie would say. It was about getting them comfortable, drawing them out, untying whatever knot they had in their heads. Whatever Jadie thought they needed to start the tour or finish the movie, or maybe the novel but there weren't so many writers, unless they were script writers, because most of the writers were from the east coast and east coast people don't really like nature, they actually kind of hate nature, because its dirty and scary and there might be bears. But after two or three days Eldon would get a text and he'd head back out to the island. And they would return to whatever Instagram-fueled hell that passed for their world. But once in a while, like tonight, Eldon needed a little attention of his own.

26

LONG AFTER ELDON had left for the island, the shift over, Amy organized her tips, leaving some for the bartender and kitchen crew. Finally hoisting her bag over her shoulder, she headed out the door into the damp evening air, her pickup towards the back of the potholed lot. She was almost to her truck when she heard a voice. One she knew but couldn't quite place. But then she knew, and she sighed. Do we really need to do this right now, she thought.

"Hey, Randy," she said.

By now he'd cornered her, back against the fence away from the parking lot lighting, and he started off sort of nice and got not so nice and she played along, dropped her eyes and gave those one syllable answers that he knew meant she would be his, one of the girls in the stable. Then he did the soft part of the close after the hard part, about to say, Hey baby, I'll take care of you, and she nods, head down as he leaned in and tried to give her a kiss. She snapped a knee into his crotch, like a two by four into a pillow, with a fist to the stomach for good measure. Gasping, he dropped to his knees as she reached behind and pulled a 9mm out of her belt. She held it along his ear and jacked a round into the chamber, moving it under his chin and pushing his head up against the chain link. By now Randy was breathing hard through his teeth and fighting the urge to puke. She leaned down, close in.

"Thanks for the offer, Randy," she said. "Lets not do this again. And say hey to your dickhead friend Cory for me."

She picked up her bag and stuffed the 9mm in the back of her jeans muttering, Stupid fucker, as she walked to her truck.

27

THE SUN WAS far in the west as he made his way through north Portland. He hit the mercado and headed over the St Johns bridge to Hwy 30, the smell of carnitas heaven filling the truck. Instead of turning left towards Portland, he turned away from the city towards the island. He crossed the span from the mainland and passed the convenience store run by the Korean family dispensing refuge parking passes and beer, chicken tenders and jojos. And he began to see it as his passengers did, a place so far away and different from LA or Silicon Valley or New York that it was a thing in your gut, a longing you never knew you had. After some time he turned the truck through the opening in the roadside brush, rumbled over the wooden bridge and broke into the clearing, the old farm house on the far side. Jadie was sitting in the big chair on the porch.

"Hey, Eldon," she said. "So glad to see you."

She walked, glided really, down the porch stairs as he climbed from the Impala.

"Wonderful you're staying and not just dropping off."

She leaned in for a hug and not just a hug but one where she breathed in, seemed to pull something out of him, and exhaled. She kept holding him until he relented and relaxed some. She wrapped an arm around his waist as they climbed onto the wide porch and in the front door. The

98

first floor was one big room with worn fir floors covered in tattered oriental rugs. Overstuffed chairs and couches were in no certain order. The kitchen was at the back of the room with an enormous and ancient enamel sink under a window that looked out at the mown hay field beyond, now settling into dusk. Along the walls of the kitchen were high shelves with rows of Mason jars, canned fruit and vegetables, dried herbs and whatever might end up in a mug. Between the two spaces sat a big oak table, as worn and comfortable as the floors.

"Have a seat, Eldon," she said and took the bag of tacos, an offering. "I'll get us plates. You need a beer?"

A beer was exactly what he needed so he said, "Yes, thanks, that would be great," as he settled into a couch, the leather cracked and soft and welcoming, this too drawing some poison.

They ate tacos and downed the beers and she asked after Amy and Betty. After a while she said, "Let's go outside. Its a beautiful evening."

The mown hay crunched underfoot as they walked into the field. She took his hand, not like a lover and not like his mother or a friend but something of all three. He hadn't tasted anything in the beer, or the tacos. But something was happening. That was OK since he couldn't imagine where he'd rather be. Some of it was her work, whatever came from those jars, and was some of it just being here, the letting go. The thought passed as they walked into the field to watch the moonrise. He could hear cows lowing in the distance as the ducks and geese muttered their goodnights across the slough. As he felt gears engage, a rattle and pull like riding the car to the top of the roller coaster, she squeezed his hand.

"Don't worry," she said. "Just go with it. I'll be here."

He stepped aside, close to her but just far enough that the air flowed around him equally which seemed to really matter at this moment. It seemed to guide his path, kept his momentum completely balanced and spinning upward. And as he arced over the top there was a falling away and emptying out like leaving a room and later, after, he couldn't construct anything like an ordering of the time. Certain moments would come to him, collapsed to no time, shattered and shuffled around and so it seemed he was still in the meadow, or back in the meadow as darkness descended and the moon rose and the meadow began to deconstruct, fractal pieces devolving to its parts, a puzzle coming apart on its own, and he could see where the pieces fit together, that they were parts of a whole but that the seams between the pieces were fraying, and there was space between them but behind the pieces was the field, another field, a less light field. And he thought Jadie was beside him but she became a little less real, a little less exactly what she was and more of something else but she remained saying nothing or maybe she was saying something and while he couldn't really make out the words, the meaning was, *I'm here, Eldon, You're safe,* and it was almost like the opposite of the other world where people say things, words, words that would have a clear meaning on the surface but you had no idea what they really meant, what was under the surface and he supposed, if required to issue an opinion, he might say they were still in the meadow but maybe a part where the grass was softer, not the hard shafts of the cut hay, but that wasn't any kind of thought he needed to have right now and Jadie was still around, not far away but another locus, nearby, but one only he could enter so she sat patiently outside the door while he sat in this new place, and another time came to him, played on background while he tried to understand the place he was in now and that memory was of Amy, in no place, just Amy with her face and her heart and he was telling her about a dream. They were swimming, far out in the ocean, or not the ocean because this place, the place in the dream was nothing but water and the water was warm and perfect and he and Amy were swimming and he dove down, deep, but alone, and there was the knowledge that Amy was above but couldn't be here among the fish and the coral and shafts of sunlight and he thought it was a wonderful and a safe place but he also knew that Amy couldn't join him here and that was okay too, and he wasn't sure how the dream ended or if that was how it ended with him just staying down there with something like contentment and he couldn't believe he told Amy about the dream anyway, not something you talked about in Paisley or Memphis but then Amy was Jadie's child and the kind of person you told those things to. Well, that's an easy one, she had said. The water, the ocean, well that's you. And you didn't have to worry about breathing right, didn't think about needing to surface, right? And he thought that was about right, that he just moved in the water, not really even swimming, just moving through it and she said, Well, that's you, Eldon, the water, its you and what you saw down there, all that beauty and wonder, well that's what's in here, as she put her fingers to his heart, and they both laughed, maybe to break a spell woven, and Amy said, That's what my mom would say anyway, and Eldon said, Yeah, whatever and signaled for another beer and then the channel changed and he was in a different space, like a room but not really a room because images of the moonlit field were there but a feeling of a room and there was a thing in the room, and he could picture it in his mind and it was in front of him too, like the border between his mind, what was in his mind and what made up the world had become porous and the thing he saw was a box, like an old stagecoach strongbox, black cast iron with rust showing, and those big rivets along the edges and a padlock the size of your hand. And he knew what was in the box and had no desire, no intention of ever opening that box, this box that sat in the back of his mind, like an old trunk in the back corner of the attic but something yanked free the rough steel of the lock and threw the iron lid back. At first nothing happened, the box was open and seemed empty but it wasn't so empty, just so dark and away at the bottom the creatures still slumbering, now waking, snuffling about, circling each other then rushing out at once; savage little things with short bristly hair and accusing eyes and claws like old dogs and stubby, mangy tails that swarmed around his feet, not attacking, just threatening with their presence, their accusation, of everyone left behind and there were other memories or something like memories of sturgeon fish rolling in the lake beyond the dyke, water steaming off their scaleless sides, glistening in the moonlight and the stars, the signal lights, tracers, between and among, talking, making sure each was in the right place in the sky and maybe towards dawn, not so dark, when things awoke and the mallard and her ducklings told him to stay there, on that side of the slough, away from the lake where the sturgeon were, stay where Jadie was but it all circled back to the creatures, his familiars, and after a while those snarling things became more like feral cats, the kind that come to your back porch for that food you're not supposed to leave out for them. With the same claws and fangs for sure, and you'd still feel them once in a while. But mostly they didn't pay you much mind while they had their Little Friskies and after a time they'd even let you pet them. So the things from the box became things he could observe without too much worry or pain or guilt, not gone but not dangerous, and this was the part he took with him, that he remembered later.

Another leap of time and the sun was up and the ground mist burned off so it might be midmorning and she asked if she could leave him, was he OK, could he navigate on his own and he thought that he could so she took his hand for a moment and kissed his cheek. Then she turned with a smile towards the farm house across the field. Some of the world was coming back to him, the shape of it and the order of it with time assuming a rhythm he knew and there was a bed of grass in the sun near the edge of the slough and the desire and the need for sleep came like it was there waiting for him.

28

ELDON SURFACED FROM a blank and dreamless place with a thought. Eyes on him. Someone, something was observing him. As the world began to assemble itself, the wind in the cottonwoods, the grass underneath, the sun on his face he thought those eyes might be part of this world. And that was OK because it seemed that the eyes, the observer, meant no harm, no malice. And so Eldon opened his.

A few feet away, at the edge of the water, sat two raccoons. Juveniles by the look of them, trying to discern this creature as something to eat, or to play with. Or to run from. Eldon sat up. They remained as they were.

"Hey there," Eldon said, his voice not quite knit back to him. "How's it going, guys?"

One with head cocked to the side, the other staring straight at him, they, with their raccoon eyes, wondering who he was and what was he doing on their bank.

"Don't worry, guys. I'll be leaving presently," he said and only when he stood, assumed some height over them did they turn and head into the brush. And he could swear they flipped him off so he laughed out loud and the laugh brought him all the way back.

Eldon climbed the bank to the edge of field. It was late afternoon but it was June and there was plenty of light left in the day which made him glad for a reason he couldn't quite name. But then the smell of bbq and maybe steak came to him with a desire like a teenage boy. Or a middle aged adulterer meeting their lover. As Eldon made his way across the field Jadie looked up from the smoke of the meal and waved. Part of him was brittle and part of him was solid and the center was solid and and the brittle part, that part was around the outside and it would knit itself back together. And what would help was whatever Jadie had going on that grill.

"Hey Eldon, just in time," she said. "Figured you might need it. And maybe these too," tossing him a pack of cigarettes.

She handed him a beer and lit his smoke. He took a long glorious drag, the smoke like the one after sex or a big meal but times a million. Exhaling, he slumped into a chair on the porch, took another pull on his beer and looked out over the field.

They sat and ate and talked and she let him bring up the last day as he might, not asking, not opening it up because she knew Eldon wasn't that guy and frankly she was glad because sometimes, God, those people could talk and she would of course let them, it was all part of the process, but being a narcissist was bad enough, let alone one that had just had their box opened up. Eldon wasn't one of those but he did talk some, let her know that he understood the gift she had given him and somewhere around his third beer the night and the day and steak worked their particular magic and it was time for bed.

"Go for it,"she said. "I'll clean up. Your room's at the top of the stairs."

It was above the kitchen with the same east view, the moon streaming in, and a bed with wooden headboard and old cotton sheets and blankets and too many pillows and when he saw it, when he laid on it, that bed was the place he had been looking for his whole life and the falling asleep was like falling off a cliff. Later that night she slipped in as the big spoon and he woke enough to know she was there but not enough to see if there was anything to be done about it.

The rain had come in overnight and pattered on the roof as he listened to Jadie moving in the kitchen, the smell of bacon and coffee making its way upstairs. After breakfast she handed over his phone.

"Maybe don't turn it on until you cross the slough," she said.

With that, she gave him a hug, then a kiss. The kind of kiss Curtis said'd make a preacher man kick in a stained glass window.

"Don't be such a stranger," she said. "Maybe stay another day next time. Maybe get a different cure."

Every time he left the farm, as he approached the bridge, he had the same thought. To stop the Chevy, dowse the bridge and torch it, to burn it to the water line leaving the piers to rot into the mud. Then to throw his keys into the slough and join Jadie in that big swinging chair on the front porch, cutting off the past and the present, all the places and people he knows, the people he knew. But he kept going until he made the pavement. When he hit the Korean market he pulled into the parking lot and turned his phone on. With pings and buzzes it came awake. There were texts from Amy and Betty, Tony and Meghan, and few others. Plus one more. From Mel.

found her

29

ELDON WALKED UP the ramp with another couple of burgers and a large fry. He thought of the orphans he'd seen in the slums of Calcutta and the stories. Of how their mothers, when they reached a certain age, the age when their youth, their cuteness no longer guaranteed success, would cut off one of their arms, or maybe blind them with battery acid so they'd have an advantage with their cup. Mel took a dollar from a commuter, "God bless you," and looked up.

"Hello kind sir," he said. "Always nice see you."

Eldon handed him the bag, plus another twenty.

The expansive lawn of Tom McCall Waterfront Park was filled with carnival rides and food booths. The smell of deep fryers mixed with the sodden lawn and stale beer. The Willamette River sea-wall was lined with ships, in for Fleet Week, some from the US Navy, others from Canada and the US Coast Guard. The promenade between the lawn and the sea-wall was busy with a lunch time assortment of runners, skaters and bicyclists weaving among gawking tourists, old bums with bad teeth and pale desk dwellers in their office clothes.

A damp breeze came off the river as the low sky gathered itself for the next shower. Rachel pulled her collar up. There was a sting as the rough cloth caught on a row of precise half inch scabs on the inside of her left wrist. Nothing serious, just practice. One for each day they had been back in Portland. Sitting near the end of the bench, in an orbit just outside the group, she could feel drops of blood form, like secret little screams. She thought that she'd kicked this little coping habit but all she had to do was look over her right shoulder and she could pick out her father's building. She could find his office window if she cared to look.

Her little band was at the north end of the park, in the hulking shadow of the Steel Bridge. Mostly young, generally homeless, their bodies adorned in tattoos and piercings. They dressed in a variation of filthy khaki and brown denim with that particular odor of much weed and little bathing. Their surplus camo backpacks, hung with patches and charms, made them look like a spent army of the apocalypse. There were a few guitars and skateboards among them, along with their dogs. Mongrels on rope leashes for protection and companionship, and attracting spare change.

She knew why they had wanted to come back to Portland. Hell, she'd loved the Rose Festival as a kid, too. But it wasn't about ferris wheels and stuffed animals. There were marks and drugs and garbage cans overflowing with half-eaten cart food. And if a girl or a boy didn't mind the work, a city full of sailors. But this was too close. The pipe came her way and, her vision fixed somewhere in the distance, she took a hit and passed it back. Brittany appeared, Chiba straining at the lease. It hopped up, with big front paws in Rachel's lap. A wet nose to an ear and a sloppy tongue.

"Ah, Chiba, come on!," Rachel laughing in spite of herself as she gently moved him off her lap and wiped her face with her sleeve.

"You little shit," she said, giving him a scratch between the ears. A shadow passed to her right and someone slid in next to her on the bench. A man.

"You're a hard girl to find."

"Huh?," she said.

The group shifted, encircling the pair. A fucking troll, trying to score some street tail. A minute's work and they'd leave him bleeding on the pavement and melt into Old Town. Ready to bolt, she turned.

But it wasn't the guy from the alley. At least not that guy.

"Matt! Holy shit!," she said. "Hey guys, it's cool. Really. I know this guy."

She turned back to Matt, a little shaky after his second brush with violence this week.

"Sorry about that," she said. "We kinda look out for each other. I had a little situation a few days ago."

Matt raised an eyebrow.

"But I guess you know about that."

"Uh-huh," he said. "Let's we take a walk, maybe get a cup of coffee? Not far, just over to Floyd's. I'll buy us some lunch. Tell your pals I'll walk you back."

He got her with the lunch part. She gave her crew a nod and they walked towards Naito Parkway and Old Town pausing for a day-care clutch to pass, with tiny hands grasping the buddy rope.

"So," Matt said, "about your little situation."

"Yeah, who was that guy anyway? The cowboy. He was a trip. Pretty lucky you guys came along though."

"Actually, we're both lucky Eldon came along."

"Eldon?," she asked. "You know that guy?"

"Well, not really. But I'm pretty sure your dad hired him to find you." Matt stepped aside, making room for a skater. "I'm still not sure what to make of him."

A cloud passed behind her eyes.

"You're not going to tell Jeffrey and Genny are you?" She'd quit calling them mom and dad a long time ago.

"Well, I hadn't gotten that far," he said. "Didn't really think I'd find you to be honest. Probably wouldn't have except for the laugh. At least that hasn't changed much."

He gave her a once over. Pale face make-up, maroon lip gloss and thick black eyeliner. Her hair was dyed, black and shaggy around her face with a shapeless felt hat, pulled low. Goth goes camping.

"Looks good on you, though," he said with a crooked smile and she punched him in the shoulder.

Floyd's sat two blocks off Front Street with brick walls, tall windows and big square timbers, the kind from one tree, like columns down the middle of the room. Old bay-windows looked out on a   courtyard. The server wasn't quite sure what to make of the middled-aged guy and the street girl but it wasn't good. Rachel was used to it, used to being either invisible or treated with some form of fear and disgust. They found a table, one of the window seats, and waited for their food. It'd been awhile since she'd had a meal that wasn't from a shelter or a trash can.

"How's Peg?," she said. "I miss you guys."

Matt looked down at his hands.

"Ah shit, Matt. I'm sorry."

Matt looked up.

"So, what about you? Are you OK? Who are those kids?"

"We hang with those other guys some. But really its me, mama and a couple of other kids; Brittany and Kyle. Our little tribe."

Rachel explained that mama, well that's what they called her anyway, was old, maybe thirty-five.

"She kind of takes care of us," she said. "She knows all the places to camp, where to get food. She used to be a teacher or something. I get the feeling we're the kids she lost somewhere."

"You should come home with me. Peg would love to see you."

He wrinkled his nose.

"She might make you burn your clothes, though," he said with a wink, but still.

"No fucking way, Matt. I'm still a minor. If Jeffrey finds out he'll put me in some kind of hospital or boot camp or something. And Genny, she's still a waste product. I think Jeffrey would be happier if I were dead and he could play the mourning father," she snorted. "It would pump up his compassion cred. Father of a dead runaway and all that."

Matt didn't reply. He wasn't sure he disagreed.

She reached across the table and touched Matt's wrist.

"Really, I've got my crew. I'm OK."

Matt looked at her knuckles, a row healing scabs.

"Oh yeah, well, stuff happens. Matt, I'll be eighteen in six months. But right now, if you tell them, or try and get me home, I'll disappear."

The food arrived and she tried not to inhale it. They left Floyd's and walked back towards the waterfront. Matt pulled a business card from his wallet, then a twenty.

"Can you text me?," he said. "Maybe lunch again tomorrow?"

"Sure," she said. "Somebody's usually got a phone. And that does sound better than dumpster diving."

As they crossed Front Street, and back to the waterfront, the breeze came up, taking the comfort of the meal and the time with Matt, with it. She wanted to be eleven again. It was all she could not to take his hand and lean into him, like when she wished Matt and Peg were her parents. He turned and put a hand on her shoulder.

"Scares the shit out of me, you out here," he said.

Rachel put on her best tough girl face.

"Matt, its cool," she said. "I'll be all right."

She gave him a hug and he hugged her back and it was the kind of hug one should get from their parents but never was.

"I just need to figure some shit out," she said.

Rachel turned and started across the lawn towards the group. Chiba caught sight of her and strained at his leash, tail wagging. Brittany dropped the tether and he bounded towards her. With one more wave to Matt she patted Chiba's side, picked up the leash and disappeared into the circle.

To anyone else on the promenade, he was just another tourist with a Nikon, photographing the waterfront, the ships, the bridges. He pulled his phone from his pocket, scrolling to Jeffrey's burner phone number. Before hitting 'call', he looked at the photos again. Eldon scratched his chin, hit 'cancel' and slid the phone back into his pocket.

30

SHE THOUGHT SHE'D need to trick them into it; not sure they'd find each other on their own. But in the end it wasn't that hard. She'd just said, Hey, let's get a beer and see some music, to both of them without mentioning the other. And so here she sat at the White Eagle pub. A deep, narrow space in an old brick building near the Union Pacific railroad yards in North Portland. The place had been built around 1905 and the upstairs was supposed to be haunted. It used to serve sailors and railroad workers and was even called the Bucket of Blood for a time. But now it was just another Portland hipster bar with rooms to rent upstairs. And since no one ever came screaming down the stairs Amy didn't think much about the haunted part. Plus her mom had been here and hadn't felt a thing. Other places sure, like when they would drive over the railroad tunnel under North Portland. Jadie would get a shiver and Amy would know what was below. But as for the pub, All I'm picking up here is desperate singles, creative facial hair and tats, Jadie had said.

Matt was the first to arrive and she got nervous. Now that he was there, she wasn't sure if this was a good idea. Matt asked her if she was OK when he came back with the beers. Yeah, she said. Just a long day. There was a blues duo tonight and she knew Eldon couldn't resist that so he'd be here too. The place was starting to fill up and she was preoccupied, watching for Eldon, and Matt asked again.

"You sure you're OK? You seem kind of jumpy," he said.

"Yeah, sure I'm fine."

She spotted Eldon at the door, half a head taller than the others, waiting to pay the cover.

"And um," she said, "I hope you don't get mad."

"Mad about what?," Matt said.

Then Eldon was beside them.

"Hey, guys," he said, with his own look of wondering.

Matt looked at Amy and said, "Now I get it."

"Get what?," Eldon said and then he looked at Amy and he got it too.

He shook his head with a little smile. "I guess I'll go get myself a beer."

Back with the beer, he gave Amy a kiss on the cheek and stuck out his hand.

"Good to see you again, Matt."

"You, too, Eldon."

They were glad to see each other but trying to navigate the water, figure their parts in Amy's little set-up but then the music started up and they let the topic slide. Some folks left and they grabbed a table up front. Amy knew the singer and they hugged and caught up. She used to dance some to make ends meet. But on this stage with that guitar and the mic is where she really belonged. Just the singer and her partner on bass but they filled the place up just fine. Too loud to talk during the music and some small talk during the breaks was about it for the three of them. Nothing about the alley or Rachel or Jeffrey. But Matt and Eldon seemed to get on well enough and Amy was glad she took the chance.

A couple of beers in, and a break in the set. Matt turned to Eldon.

"Can I ask you a question?"

"Sure," Eldon said.

"That day in the alley, when you showed up. That wasn't an accident was it?"

"Not exactly, no," Eldon said.

"Jeffrey then." Matt said.

Eldon, looking toward the stage, gave a slow nod.

On towards midnight, Matt said, "Oh man, I gotta grab a ride. Work tomorrow."

As he got up Eldon said, "Hey, you said you played some harp, right? Any good?"

"Yeah," he said. "I guess I'm alright. I'm a one trick pony but I'll do OK as long as we stick to the blues."

"You want to come by my place and jam some?," Eldon said. "I've been rusty. Need some playing time. And maybe we talk about the other thing and maybe don't. But let's play some."

There was a pause and Matt was waiting for the little voice to say it was a bad idea and not to trust this guy but the voice was silent.

"Yeah, that'd be cool. Been too long."

31

HE STOPPED IN a Starbucks on NW 21st to use the internet connection. Coffee in hand Cory grabbed a table, opened the laptop and fired up the encrypted browser. If they only knew, Cory thought as his keystrokes bounced around the world, finally landing in a basement in Kiev. That last batch of roofies seemed to be made of talcum powder and he needed a new supplier. Next to him, a homeless guy sat, scribbling in a notebook, with three empty and somewhat battered to-go cups arranged in front of him.

Eldon had met Curt when he first drifted into town. He'd used him for some tailing and other odd jobs. But the street and all that came with it, was beginning to drag him down. Now it looked way past beginning. Today, Curt sat with three empty, and somewhat battered Starbucks cups. He believed the cups would lend legitimacy to his presence. *Look! I bought three drinks!* His brown and stained overcoat slung over the chair, he hunched close over some notebook paper, his glasses lost in a drinking bout some months ago. If it wasn't for his ratty shoes, he could almost be just another Portland hipster. Almost. But the shoes always give it away. His filthy hands clutched a ball point pen. He peered intently, closely, at the paper, adding a few words here and there. He'd been trying to write his mother for weeks. No way is he going to call her. Too hard, too much baggage. But a note, that would be good. Let her know he's OK, give her something to hang on to. Some days he really feels like he's going to get started, get a plan to get off the street. He knows some guys that start the climb selling that newspaper, Street Roots. But then he would run out of medication, or sell it for something more invigorating and feel lost again, find himself in a bottle. But today, rather than write, he's drawing the creatures that give him solace. Small dinosaurs, giant squirrels and the other entities that inhabit his comic book world. He left two of the cups at the table, and carried the third outside to smoke the half cigarette he found earlier in the day. If he kept his eyes open and didn't go through them too quickly, he found plenty of smokes. In fact, he'd gotten to where he couldn't see buying them. But how could he anyway? With the taxes, a pack was pushing seven dollars. Too bad half-full bottles weren't as common. Oh, yeah, he thought, a task. He fished a phone from his pocket and stared at it for a moment. Then, eyes close to the screen, he pecked at it with an index finger, almost spelling the words right. Back at the table, the odor of many cigarettes and little bathing drifting to the other customers, he started back on his story. After few more intent scribbles, his radar comes on. A Portland cop in for his morning cup. Curt really hasn't really done anything. Except smell bad. And not spent any money which, in America, is the real crime. The cop looked about, relaxed. In fact, he didn't look at the Curt at all. But Curt's warning bells are clanging in his head. He pulled on his overcoat, gathered his notebook and headed out the door, the three cups left behind.

Cory pulled his cap down a bit but otherwise ignored the cop. And glad that the man, and his smell, had gone. Cory went back to work. A minute later, the cop left as well. As he typed away a tall man in a cowboy hat sat in the chair opposite.

"Cory Stalmer, you're a hard man to find."

Cory closed the laptop.

"And who the fuck are you?"

"Eldon Truly," holding out his hand.

Cory looked at it like it was a dead cat. Eldon dropped the hand, and the smile.

"Listen Cory, seems you've taken an interest in a certain young lady," Eldon said. "I'm here to say that you're interest is misplaced. Might be best to look elsewhere."

"I don't know what you're talking about dickhead," Cory said. "Now get out of my face before I stick that hat up your ass."

Eldon gave a little smile, tipped the Stetson and went out the door.

32

THEIR CAMP WAS just south of downtown close to the river. The Marquam Bridge loomed and the roar of freeway traffic washed down. Rachel, Kyle and Brittany sat close to the small fire in its circle of light and heat. In the shadows outside the fire light, Mama curled in her sleeping bag working off whatever opiate she'd scored that day.

"Damn," Kyle said, "I'm sick of these little fires. Can't we build a real fire some time?"

Rachel had only to think of the sound of her bedroom door opening, late in the evening, to know why she was camped under this bridge. The rest had their own versions. Kyle was a big kid, doughy like a football player that didn't play anymore. The high carb meals at the shelters weren't doing him any favors. He'd been an offensive lineman at an eastern Washington high school until he got caught with a teammate in the shower. Neither the town nor his family was quite ready for that so Kyle made his way to Portland after his father kicked him out. Brittany had come from a small town on the Oregon coast. She was birdlike; blond and skinny and cute, but with a hardness around the eyes. Rachel's father and Brittany's uncle shared certain traits although they differed in that Brittany's uncle was down a testicle. Kyle had the size. But Brittany, a folding knife in her back pocket, was the enforcer in the tribe.

Brittany scratched a lottery ticket.

"Nothing, damn," she said and threw it into the fire.

The shiny ticket, twisting in the heat, gave up a green blue flame, its tiny bit of hope going up with the smoke. A joint, a wine bottle and a 2 lb bag of shoplifted Ruffles went around the circle.

"Let's do something tomorrow, I'm fucking bored," Brittany said as she blew out the hit and passed the joint to Rachel.

"Some kind of adventure," she said. "I wish we could go to the beach or something. There were some cool caves we'd explore when I was little."

Brittany took the bottle and tipped it back.

"They were kind of secret," she said. "You could only get to them with a really low tide. We used to imagine pirates had used them or maybe Indians for secret rituals."

They fell silent but for the crackle of the fire and Kyle's chip bag.

"I know where there's a secret cave," Rachel said. "Here. In Portland. We could check it out."

"What do you mean, a secret cave?," asked Kyle.

"Well, more like a secret chamber. At least I think there's one," Rachel said. "I found some drawings, and a map, in my dad's office, at our house. My family's been in the same house since like nineteen hundred. There's papers and stuff going back to my great grandfather. I thought they were old and really cool. Yellowed maps, old hand drawn construction plans, photos, shit like that. It was like my own museum. And this one time, in the bottom of an old file drawer I found this leather folder."

She'd found some other things, too. A small digital camera and some memory cards. Nothing as interesting as the drawings and diagrams though.

"It had a bunch of plans and drawings," she said," a thick fancy door with all these gears and weights inside and some kind of chamber, the writing all in Chinese, except for a few notes, maybe written by my grandfather. The door had this weird lock, a circle about as big as your hand, of seven fingered sized holes. Pretty sure I still remember the pattern There's this super long railroad tunnel under the city."

"Uh-uh, sure," said Brittany.

"Yeah," Rachel said, "on the other side of the river. It goes from up north of the city, underneath it, and comes out under the bluff near the college over there. My great grandfather helped build it. I guess he built a lot of things around here about a hundred years ago, bridges, roads. Anyway, I found this secret chamber stuff with all the tunnel files."

Mama stirred and sat up, blinking.

"Ah, the secret hideout of William Barton," she said, rubbing her eyes. "Could you pass me the bottle, Rachel?"

She took a drink, wiping her mouth on the back of her wrist.

"You're a Barton, aren't you, sweetie?"

Mama's full name was Sarah Marie Thornton, Ms. Thornton to her students. She had been a history teacher at David Douglas High School. She loved her subject and she loved her students. Ms. Thornton thought textbooks were useless so she'd bring in old books and atlases, huge tomes borrowed from the historical society. She never used a roller cart to tote her books and materials and laptop from the car. Thought they were for old ladies. She'd swing her hefty messenger bag over one shoulder and head to her classroom. Somewhat predictably, Ms. Thornton developed a bulging disk. The Advil and a glass of wine turned to Vicodin and bourbon then Oxy. And when that got hard to find it turned to heroin. When she started getting it from one of her students it didn't take long for that rumor to find its way home. And then she wasn't a teacher anymore. The downward spiral tightened until it spit her out on to the street. She'd been on and off, mostly on, for close to ten years now. No more books to carry, leisure time of a sort, and sleeping on the hard ground had cured her back. The addiction was tougher. But her love of the kids was still there. Just different kids. And that's how she found herself the semi guardian to three lost teenagers. She could lie in her own urine for the better part of a day but ask her a question about local history and she would pull herself up, a light in her eyes. And as she slipped into her former self, her teacher self, her eyes cleared and her posture straightened. With a small slur she began.

"Well, Miss Barton, your father didn't fall too far from the tree," mama said. "Your great great grandfather, William Barton, was a first citizen of Portland from last century. He arrived in Portland about 1890 and started a construction company. By 1900 the Willamette and the Columbia were going to be the gateway for the logs and wheat and beef of the Northwest. Portland grew, and you know in its heyday it was bigger than the little city of Seattle, and it was an open city. None of this squeaky clean government like today. The story goes that he had three or four brothels, paid off the police in money, women and opium. He used to run girls and Chinese labor and opium down river and up and down the west coast. Many of Portland's finer families dabbled in all that as well. But most of them decided to go straight, build a school or a church or give money to the symphony. Launder the money, and their good names, as it were. I'd say your family didn't see the need."

She stopped and motioned to Brittany for the bottle.

"He paid off the right people and he got the big contracts - the ones for the bridges, the railroads and tunnels. Like this one. Today, no one knows about it. But back then, the Peninsula tunnel was a big deal. A mile long tunnel right under the city. It took two years and a hundred men. A lot of it Chinese labor."

Mama paused, the fire flickering on her face.

"Once they got down through the dirt," she said, "it was fifteen feet a day through solid basalt; dynamite and dust and bad air. No telling how many died in there. But you can imagine it, back there in the dark, their carbide lamps castings ghostly shadows, the white foremen back aways, out of the blast zone, back where the air was better, *Let the Chinamen do it*, they'd said, *They don't mind*, and so they'd set the charges and their ears would ring until they didn't at all and they'd clear away the rock and the rubble, light beams through the dust, in their eyes, in their lungs, pile the spoils into the carts and haul them, squinting, out into the light, and they'd turn around and head back in while the foremen smoked their cigars and yelled, *Chop chop!* laughing. Today its all industrial land but back then the tunnel emptied into a swamp. The elevated tracks ran through a scow town -

tarpaper shacks on waterlogged rafts, rickety house boats and grounded fishing trawlers connected by plank bridges and rope slings. The only time Portland's Finest appeared was to visit a whorehouse or pick up a bribe, or maybe a body. They say the last of Portland's opium dens were down there. It makes sense that he'd connect with the Chinese. There were pretty close to ten thousand here then. Stuck to themselves, didn't speak the language. A great cover if you could get inside the circle. Remember, the Chinese had a complex society before the West was potty trained. The craftsman that built that door would have been standing on thirty generations of accumulated knowledge. And, the seven holes would make sense, hon. Its one of the few numbers that's considered lucky in both western and Chinese culture."

The bottle came her way again. Mama scratched her haunches and took a long swallow. Kyle, Brittany and Rachel sat wide eyed, like cub scouts hearing a ghost story.

"And the location, too," mama said. "It wasn't too far from the river bank then. A good crossroads for the river traffic and north south railroad line - the mainline between the NW and California. Easy enough to move opium, prostitutes and Chinese labor from the rails to the river. But whatever it cost, and it was a lot at the time, there was plenty enough for Mr. William Barton to skim and make his pay-offs. Who knows what's in there."

"Holy shit, mama," Rachel said. "So you think its real?"

"Could be, could be."

With that, mama's eyes unfocused and she yawned.

"Night, my babies," she said and rolled back into her sleeping bag.

In the end, hangovers, scrounging for food, the weather and a million other things got in the way and they never made it. But the next night they had another idea and since it wasn't so far and didn't involve money for bus tickets or schedules they thought this one might work.

Brittany looked at maybe two hundred geese, munching and shitting their way across the lawn of Waterfront Park, at the south end near the hotel.

"Goddamn," she said, "I'm sick of shelter food and scraps. Let's kill one of those fuckers and make supper."

The birds were near extinction thirty years ago and there was an outcry, then speeches, then laws and now the damn things were everywhere. For anyone who had to live around them, cleaning up their shit all the time, the love affair was definitely over.

"Yeah," Brittany said, "the trickiest part will be keeping it quiet, keeping the rest of them quiet til we can get its neck broken."

"I believe you're serious, young lady," mama said.

"As a heart attack. We used to keep chickens and geese and shit on the farm. Ringing its neck, that's the easy part. Damned if I know what to do with them after that. Can't cook for shit."

"Oh, I know what to do," Rachel said. "Its easy."

"Go on, Rachel," mama said.

"Well," she said," my parents would leave me with some nanny while they traveled and I'd get tired of eating from the freezer or the phone. Plus they would always send me off to these camps, cooking camps sometimes. So yeah, I know what to do."

Which was a better way to say, Yeah, I'm a pretty good cook, or even a damn good cook and she might say that to herself sometimes, quietly, and people sure as hell said it to her. But there was no way she was going to say it out loud.

"If we're going to all this trouble, we're going to do it right," she said. So Rachel gave everyone their assignments and they scattered into the city. And even though none of them said anything about it, or even could put it into words, they were grateful for the distraction of sitting around, thinking about the next bottle or fix.

One by one, they straggled back to camp with their haul, presenting it to Rachel for her perusal and, hopefully, approval. From her layers of coats and sweaters mama produced potatoes and carrots and salt and pepper while Kyle hefted a 20 lb bag of charcoal from his shoulder. Rachel gave him a, How'd you pull that off look.

"Mama faked one of her coughing fits and I just grabbed the bag and ran," he said.

Brittany tossed out two split pieces of oak swiped from the back of a wood fired pizza joint.

"Perfect. We won't need much, just for the smoke," Rachel had said. "Oh man, nice work guys."

Finally, she pulled out two bottles of red wine, stashed from the Council Crest run, to the oohs and ahs of her mates.

They did it that night, the taking, while the birds were asleep, dreaming their goose dreams. They picked one out near the edge of the group. Kyle crept up with a blanket, all of them trying not to laugh. In a burst he was on it, tossing the blanket, wrapping it up. The huge bird flapped and flailed and squawked, trying to work its head loose, the beak full of teeth. The rest of birds woke up with an unholy din and when the head and neck came out of blanket, searching for purchase in flesh.

Kyle started screaming, "Oh fuck, oh fuck, oh fuck."

"Jesus Kyle," Brittany hissed, "hold still for second."

She reached out, and quick as that, wrenched it's neck and it was silent. Run!, mama said and and they did, Kyle clutching the limp bundle down to the brush by the river while the other geese made *What the hell was that?* noises, then gossiped for a bit, finally muttering their geese goodnights and settling in.

Back at camp they laid open the blanket, admiring their prize.

"A beautiful animal," Mama said.

"Yeah, well its gonna be real beautiful all roasted up," Brittany said looking at Rachel. "But the first thing we gotta do is get it cleaned, she said. We got to get its guts out or it'll taste like shit, no matter how good Rachel is."

Brittany pulled the buck knife out of her back pocket and set to work while Rachel started on the veggies and Kyle on the fire. Mama settled back and read aloud from Sometimes a Great Notion.

That evening they finished the last of the meal as the city lights shimmered on the river. Tomorrow they would wake up, damp and cold. Another day on the street. But tonight, as they gnawed on the bones, these four souls shared the best meal in the city of Portland.

<h1 style="text-align:center">33</h1>

MATT WOULD BE here soon so Eldon picked up a bit. Not that the place needed it. But he did like his guitars just so. Especially that one, the one on the left. The chrome steel resonator that had belonged to Curtis..

Eldon's grandma owned a building in Memphis, a big, old house divided into four units, two up, two down. There was a deep porch shaded by the overhanging second story that faced the street. Eldon and his grandmother lived in the top right unit. Curtis in the left. He had skin like black coffee with a bit of cream, his hair cut close to the scalp, more gray than black with ropey arms and big hands. He drove bus for the Memphis Transit Authority. Then there was another guitar there on the porch, Eldon thought his grandmother bought it but never found out. It just sort of appeared one day.

"Hey, Eldon," he said. "You look like you're following along. Pick up that guitar there, I'll run you through a few chords."

And that's where it started.

"Here now," Curtis said, "get your fingers around that neck right. You gotta choke it, grab on to that thing. You want those notes to ring out. That's your practice for now, run those three cords over and over. Just think about the sound. Hear how it rings out when you've got a good hold on that neck, got those strings down hard? Otherwise, its gets all muddy, doesn't know what note it wants to be. Once you get those single notes down, you can start messing around in the middle, in between the notes. There's parts in between notes just as important as the notes themselves. How long you hold the note, do you jump right to the next one? Or, do you just kinda slide on over, maybe even let it get quiet in between."

Eldon would watch, thinking about how he wanted those notes to come, willing his fingers to get to the right spot. For the first couple of weeks it hurt like a son of a bitch, even bled sometimes. His grandmother would bundle over, tell him to quit that foolishness. But Curtis would glance over with the slightest nod, a corner of his mouth turned up. Enough for Eldon to practice for another hour.

But Curtis couldn't talk for too long before he'd have to start in. Not that Eldon minded. Curtis playing that steel guitar was the most beautiful thing he had ever heard. After while, Eldon could play the rhythm part while Curtis would come in and out of the rhythm with the lead, the wailing and pleading and crying over the beat. Curtis wasn't a bad singer either. But he'd sing just enough to call it a song. Sometimes, the best times, Nate would come by with his harps. And Eldon tried a bit of harp, loved the sound but not enough to leave the guitar sitting for too long. But the harp really did close the loop, filled in just the right spots. The wail of Carl's Hohner Special 20 going back and forth, call and response with Curtis's steel. And then after while, it was the three of them, Eldon's rhythm as the foundation, Curtis' lead rolling back and forth between Eldon's line and

Nate's harp. After while Eldon got a picture in his mind, the rhythm, an ocean swell, up and down along the bass line, nice and regular, Curtis following the line, in sync, then breaking away, swinging in tight or out wide. But always in line with the basic roll. Eldon saw the gaps in the swell, the holes that Nate would fill in. Each of them knew just when to jump in, when to let the next guy take over, a rhythm to that as well as the song, like a larger outside arc, still tied to the same current. Eldon saw Curtis glance over at Nate, then to him.

"Take it, E."

And he took his first swing outside the arc, the notes, not going too far, swinging back in time for Nate to pick up the line, his turn at the wheel. Nate looked over, nodded to Eldon and Curtis, not looking up.

"Nice, E."

Matt dropped out of the West Hills, picked up the 405 near PSU and headed towards North Portland. He parked in front of Eldon's small bungalow, chirped his car lock and rapped on the front door. It opened and Eldon held out a hand.

"C'mon in," he said. "Get you a beer?"

Matt wasn't sure what he had expected but this wasn't it. He sat a six pack and his harp case on the coffee table and took in the front room; spare with exposed wood, little furniture and a few carpets over fir floors. The word Zen occurred to him.

One wall was floor to ceiling shelves, about one third books, the rest taken up by LPs and CDs. In front of the shelves, sat Eldon's guitars, each in its own stand. Two acoustics, maybe Gibsons or a Taylor, and another one. Curtis had called, the Voice of God. The National Steel. Not a lap steel like the country guys played. It had regular guitar shape with a chrome body and ornate round vents on the front, like speakers. Even if you didn't know the name, you knew the sound. Behind him, Matt heard Eldon crack a beer, then another. He handed Matt a bottle.

"Nice guitar," Matt said pointing at the chrome body.

Eldon gazed at it like a lover.

"Yeah, that one was Curtis's. He was Black, about my grandma's age. They had a thing but didn't make too much of it. They'd both gotten to the point where they liked having someone around but were done with the rest of the complications. He'd sit out there with his old Gibson or the National Steel and play, shout out to his friends, keep an eye on the neighborhood. Sometimes a few others'd come by with a few beers or a jug of homemade and they'd jam, blues and gospel. Sometimes Grandma would sing along with one of the gospel tunes. But it was the blues stuff that pulled me in. *A distant and richer cousin* someone said once to the country music I grew up with."

They were silent for moment, admiring the chrome body.

"Curtis used to call it the voice of God," Eldon said. "You brought your harps, right?," he said. "Well, get 'em out. Let's play."

They were into it for a couple of hours, a few more beers and a couple of joints and Matt said, "Well, its not hard to guess where we'd fall on the Stones or Beatles question, eh?"

Eldon laughed and said, "No, I guess not. Now, don't get me wrong. I'm not questioning their place in musical or cultural history. But yeah, he said, its mostly pop and just not my thing."

"I hear you," Matt said. "But if you really want to liven up a party just casually drop that you don't like the Beatles. That'll get folks riled up for sure. And, don't even get me started on the Who, the whole Tommy bullshit. Rock opera? Give me a fucking break. But then they were started by a couple guys with opera and classical musical backgrounds anyway."

"That so?," Eldon said. "Well, that explains a lot."

"Right?," Matt said. "See what I mean. There's no groove to it, just the bang bang bang of white people music. And I realize we're just a couple of white guys sitting here but that shit just doesn't work for me."

"Yeah," Eldon said, "Curtis had his own theory about all that. He said it went all the way back to the beginning, before there were humans. Something about the rhythm of the universe, back to the big bang or something like that and, well, the first people, they came out of Africa, and we all knew that, and that if you think about it, we are descended from that band, the original band, Lucy or what ever you want to call it. So the Chinese and the Eskimos and the Polish and the Russians, all of us came from that band that came out of the Rift valley, like the earth opened up and they came out, from somewhere near the origin of the universe, when the earth came out of the dust that formed the galaxy and then the sun, the circles, the spirals that formed into the galaxies, and then the stars and then the solar systems and then the planets, all starting form the same spiral set in motion at the beginning and circle kept spinning and the ground opened and the first people came out and it was in Africa and well we call them black people and they are different, black, not like us, and they've paid for that almost from the beginning, but the music, the blues, and here's what he really wanted to get at, the blues, jazz and before that, the music of Africa, well, that music is from the beginning, the beginning of the universe and when Ice Cube says its all rock and roll and when Jack White, an idiot savant connected to some cosmic shit on his own, when he says that it all goes back, like a freight train back to the blues, that's what he's talking about."

Matt, red eyed, stared back at Eldon.

"Whoa."

They pondered that for a moment.

"OK, what about Rachel?," Eldon said. "I've got this client, your friend or something."

"Or something," Matt said.

"And he hired me to find her but he doesn't seem all that interested, like he's going through the motions or something. And there's the mom."

"Genny," Matt said.

"Right, Genny. And I can't figure her out for shit. So I've got a client I can't figure out, a girl on the street who someone seems like they're trying to kill. But she'd rather stay out there then go home."

"And then," Eldon said, "there's you."

"So, you want to know about Jeffrey and I. Yeah, there's some history there. I've never told anyone this story, not even Peg. Our dad's worked together and we both went to Cathedral High. Kind of grew up together. Not sure my dad liked him much, but he was a hell of a lawyer. But yeah, Jeffrey was good looking, always had a new car and plenty of drugs. Needless to say, Jeffrey was a chick magnet. I mean, he was an asshole, but he had it all. And when he wasn't being too much of an asshole, he would share. We're in downtown Portland one winter night; chilly, wet, probably 2am. Too much coke and weed to remember. We're in his Beemer, way too fast on Naito, they called it Front Street back then, down by the river. The music's loud, singing to Nirvana or something and, shit, there he is. Right in the head lights. Some homeless guy, BAM, onto the hood, the windshield and over the car, just like that. Jeffrey locked 'em up and we skid to a stop, sideways in the street. We can see that the guy is trying to get up. I can hardly believe it but he's alive. I start to get out, to see if the guy's OK. Well, shit. He wasn't OK, but I'm just thinking we need to help. But Jeffrey's screaming at me."

"Get in the fucking car!"

"Huh? But we need to .. "

"Matt get in the fucking car right now! For christ sake, he's just a homeless guy. Practically jumped in front of us. Now get in the goddamn car and lets roll!"

"Numb, fucked up, scared. I, I got in the car and Jeffrey blew the scene. No idea what happened to the guy. Two weeks later, he's got the car back, good as new. We never brought it up again. So after college and everything, we're both married, and Portland's a small town so we see each other around and our wives hit it off. And life's funny, you know. Peg can't have kids and I won't lie, its been tough for us. But Genny had Rachel and it seemed pretty clear to us that the kid was merely an accessory for them. So Rachel started hanging out with us, like her second family. But not long after that rafting trip Jeffrey took a job in DC and we didn't see them for a few years. When they got back to Portland, Jeffrey was busy, Genny disappeared into some kind of fog - alcohol and meds, I guess, and Rachel kept her distance. We were disappointed, of course. But with Rachel we just chalked it up to her being a teenager. But maybe there was something else. Jesus."

"I saw you guys on the waterfront. The day you connected with Rachel," Eldon said.

Matt wasn't sure how to take that. Eldon supposedly worked for Jeffrey but as far as he knew, he hadn't told him anything.

Eldon read Matt's face. "Yep, I took pictures of you guys. Thought about my client. Thought about you, and Rachel. And here we sit."

"So, what do we do?," Matt said.

They talked some more and came up with the start of a plan.

"OK," Matt said, "which one of us asks Amy?"

Eldon reached for his phone, tapping out a text. A moment later, a reply.

"OK, she'll meet us for lunch tomorrow."

34

AMY WAS RUNNING late so they got their coffee and sat down. Matt brought the cup to his lips.

"What the fuck," he said. "Can we ever get over this light roast shit?"

Eldon laughed. "Well there's another thing we agree on besides the Beatles."

"Its like eating a green banana," Matt said, "this under roasted shit. But don't ever say anything to the barista. They'll just look down their nose at you. *Coffee shaming*, Peg calls it."

Amy pushed through the door, a white smear across one cheek.

"Sorry I'm late, guys. I'm down a drywaller."

She peeled off a dusty canvas coat, eying them both as she sat down.

"OK, what's up? This doesn't feel like social call."

"Well," Eldon said, "we've got a little situation. And we're hoping you might be able to help."

"Mm-hmm," Amy said, clearly suspicious.

"There's this street kid. Rachel," Matt cut in. "Her name's Rachel. I've known her since she was a kid. Peg and I are her godparents actually, and she's having a rough time. She ran away, living on the street. And for reasons maybe we won't go into right now, she can't go home."

"But there's some other shit happening, too," Eldon said. "Ever heard of a guy named Cory Stalmer? Sounds like pimping strippers is one of his many lines of business," he said.

"Sure," Amy said, "I know Cory. Most of the girls know Cory. At least heard of him. I don't know why, must have been high, or thought it was another angle on me like I was some kind of challenge, but he even told me how he does it once. He'll scope the girls, see which ones have a certain look, like a certain vulnerability, and wait til they're up at the bar. He'll chat them up a bit and then tell them to buy him a drink. Most just laugh and couple tell him to fuck off but others will 'do what they're told' and he'd have another one. Me and the other girls would try and warn them off but some girls, something about their shitty childhoods or something, they just end up with guys like that. But," Amy said, "no doubt, that guy is creepy as shit."

"So, yeah," Eldon said. "We'd like to get her off the street. We're hoping you might be able to, um, help out."

"Help out, exactly how?," Amy said.

"Maybe she could stay with you," Eldon said. "Just for few days. Until we figure a couple things out."

"Jesus Christ," Amy said, "what am I, some kind of social service agency? Amy's Home for Wayward Girls, or some shit?"

But Eldon knew this was just Amy, that she needed to vent, and he turned up a corner of his mouth.

"Fuck you, Eldon Truly," she said. "OK, fine. But I need to meet her first."

Matt texted the last number he had from Rachel.

"Hope this works," he said. "I really don't want to have to go find her."

A few minutes later, his phone pinged.

"Great," Matt said, "she'll meet me for lunch at Floyds. Might be best if I don't mention you guys until we get there."

Matt and Rachel were halfway through their burritos as Eldon and Amy walked up.

"Hey Rachel? I want you to meet a couple of people."

Rachel looked up, eyes wide, ready to bolt.

"Matt," she said," I told you."

Matt held up his hand. "Don't worry, they're friends. Really, you can trust them. Have a seat guys."

Eldon and Amy sat down while Rachel looked at Matt, not happy.

"Rachel, this is Amy. And this is Eldon."

Matt waited a moment to see if the light went on. It did.

"Hey wait!," she said, "you're the guy from the alley. What the fuck, do you guys know each other?"

Now Rachel looked more confused than wary. The cowboy was at least part savior.

"Well," Matt said, "we didn't then but we do now. But the person I really want you to meet is Amy."

With the introduction made, Matt and Eldon excused themselves. Fifteen minutes later, Matt got the text.

Its cool. She's a good kid. I'm in.

35

AMY COLLECTED RACHEL, with her pack thrown in the bed of the pickup, and rolled east, across the river towards her apartment off Hawthorne Blvd. Amy buzzed herself in the front door, holding it for Rachel.

"After you, kid. Third floor."

After climbing the stairs, Amy rattled her keys for the right one and pushed open the door.

"Ok girl, the first thing that needs to happen is a shower. And give me your clothes. I'll get 'em in the wash, if they don't try and run away first, that is."

She looked Rachel up and down.

"And kick that stuff out in the hall when you peel it off. I'll get that in the wash, too. I got something here you can wear."

After her shower, a clean and scrubbed Rachel emerged in a towel.

"Hey Amy," she said, "about those clothes."

"Down here, hon, Amy said from the kitchen.

In one corner stood a compact washer/dryer stack, Rachel's stuff on the floor. She dumped the armload with the rest and Amy's eyes went to Rachel's left wrist, the row of scars. She raised an eyebrow.

"Hey, hon?," Amy said, "Do we need to talk about those?"

"Oh, right," Rachel said. "Forgot. Well, I had a few bad days. But I'm better now."

"Well, let me know," Amy said. "That ain't good."

"I promise," Rachel said.

Amy pulled the clean load from the dryer, warm clothes tumbling into the hamper. Amy dug around and and handed Rachel a t-shirt and some sweats.

"Wow," Rachel said, "you've got some pretty fancy underwear."

"Right," Amy said. "OK, so it doesn't come up later, I'll just tell you. I'm a dancer, aka a stripper. I've got a shift tonight, probably home around midnight. You gonna be okay here, by yourself?"

"Oh my god, yes," Rachel said. "Your place is awesome."

"Alright then," Amy said, "I need to eat before I roll. You hungry? "

After dinner, while Amy got ready for her shift, Rachel sat curled on the couch sipping tea, chai with a bit of milk and honey. The cardamom aroma hung in the room. All so civilized after weeks on the street.

"So, what's it like?," Rachel said. "I mean being naked in front of all those strangers?"

Amy laughed.

"People always wonder about what I do, but they never know how to ask about it. But you just did."

It Amy's turn to sip some tea,

"Yeah, so?," Rachel said.

"You know," Amy said, "I get all the feminist stuff about exploitation, degrading your body and all that. And the way it is for a lot of the girls, I get it. There's some fucked up shit in their background, shitty childhoods and everything.

But for me, to be honest, there's some real power in it too. I mean, being naked in front of men, or anyone for that matter doesn't really bother me. Shit, I spent half my growing up naked at the commune."

"Just a sec," Rachel said, "you grew up on a commune? Like hippies and stuff?"

"Yeah," Amy replied, "a story for another time. Anyway, when the music's just right, when I pick a solid tune stack and I'm feeling it, those poor guys are mine. They'd sign over their car for an hour at the rack with me. Now, I'm always super clear about where I'm coming from - usually I tell them I'm a lesbian. And boy does that work, especially for a certain type of Portland guy. The sensitive ones that are feeling guilty about being there in the first place. SNAGs right? - Sensitive New Age Guys. First of all, the lesbian thing, that I might be getting it on with another chick - 'hot girl on girl action' is what the websites say, I think, that gets them going right there. So you got them even more excited about while simultaneously shutting them down, cause hey, I don't like men, right? And then they want to be all liberal and pro-gay. Believe me, there are plenty of assholes out there. But I get their bullshit whether or not I'm naked in front of them. Its usually the guys with a pick-up truck, those big boob silhouette things on their mud flaps. But most of those guys are scared of girls anyway. And if they start up with the 'show me your cunt' stuff I just move on. Other girls put up with it, but I don't. I make enough money for the clubs I work that the management usually doesn't put up with it either."

"Yeah, but the money's pretty good isn't?"

"Well, it is right now but it took a awhile to get there. But its a means to an end," she said, glancing towards her tool bag and dusty Carhartt coat by the door. "And some people wonder why I still do it. My mom's actually pretty loaded. She lives out on Sauvie Island. Its a pretty amazing place. I'll take you out there some time. We're doing OK now but let's just say we have a complicated relationship."

"I get that one," Rachel said, taking another sip.

"But yeah," Amy said, "on a good night I can pull twelve hundred bucks. When its a bunch of regulars and I'm splitting shifts with my friends, its actually pretty fun. But, some of those Friday nights, when the bachelor parties are in and the money's just raining down on the stage like snow its pretty amazing. Its like I'm making it with nothing, literally nothing but my wits. I am naked, completely exposed, completely alone - and for a little while, I have all those little men in the palm of my hand. One of my friends, a role model really, wrote a memoir about it. Viva Las Vegas. Well, not her real name actually. But her book's called The Magic Garden. That place is gone, god rest its soul, but we dance together at Mary's. And there's Sheila and Sky and Bree and Midnight. Most girls have stage names. But we all have a pretty good time.

"But wait," Rachel said. "I want to hear more about the commune."

"You don't mind asking questions do you, kid?"

"Well, yeah. You don't have to answer if you don't want to."

"Well," Amy said, "it was more of a dope growing co-op. But pretty much a commune, yeah." adding, with a small shudder, "Like I said, a story for another time"

36

MATT WAS BACK at Eldon's. The music was really coming together. They brought around the finish to *Early in the Morning*, Matt's vibrato on the harp mixing just right with the last notes from Eldon's National steel.

"Oh yeah," Matt said.

"Indeed," Eldon said and they clinked bottles.

"Damn, we should find a gig don't you think? Maybe an open mic somewhere," Matt said. "That'd be fun."

"Oh no, not for me. I generally don't like to be that noticed. Besides, there's some serious stage fright going on here."

"Stage fright?," Matt said. "Jeez, I finally found something that spooks you."

"Oh, there are a few things," Eldon said.

Eldon usually had a better plan than this one. Or had one at all. But he needed to put some pieces together now that Rachel was off the street. Right now, it would be her word against Jeffrey's. Drug addled street kid against one of the most respected and powerful men in the city. Eldon didn't like her odds. Frankly, Eldon was wondering why he had hired him in the first place since he wasn't sure Jeffrey wanted her found. Matt figured Genny had insisted on it. Then Matt and Eldon put the pieces together after his job for the artist. A friend of Genny's. Portland was a small town. And where did Randy and this guy Cory come in? With all the kids on the street, why the interest in this girl? Something didn't make sense. Maybe some windshield time, a little change in scenery, would help. Plus, he had something to take care of.

"Hey Matt," Eldon said, "now that Rachel's off the street, feel like taking a little road trip with me? I need to take care of something. Might be two or three days."

"I don't know. What are you thinking?"

"Its my family's old place, a small ranch outside of Paisley, Lake County. You know Paisley?"

"I do, but I thought you were a Memphis boy. What do you have going on in eastern Oregon? But yeah, been out there many times. Amazing country. And there's a hot springs out there."

"Indeed there is," said Eldon. "Summer Lake Hot Springs. Used to go there when I was a kid. That bath house still there?"

"Yeah, its still there. So, you know Duane?"

"Naw, I knew the family that owned it before. But I heard he's done a nice job with the place."

"Shit," Matt said, "I knew you said your parents were passed but I didn't know you came from out there. You never quit surprising me. And I'd love to go, but I've got to work."

"What the hell," Eldon said. "Didn't you say your dad started the place, that its the family company or something? What the fuck, they going to fire you?"

"Yeah, you're right," Matt said. "Truthfully, they won't even notice I'm gone."

He sank the last of the bottle and reached for another one.

"Fuck it, let's go," Matt said. "What the hell do I carry this thing around for anyway?," he said, brandishing his phone. "I'll just need to let Peg know. We could both probably use a couple of day's space."

"I'm not sure what kind of condition the trailer's in," Eldon said. "Sounds like the last renters did a number on it. That's what I need to check on anyway.

"One more thing," he said, looking at Matt's polo shirt and khakis.

"Lose the country club shit. You got any old jeans and sneakers, maybe some t-shirts? I don't need to be seen in my home town with the some Portland liberal. You'll ruin my reputation."

Matt laughed. "I hear you," he said. "I won't embarrass you."

"OK, then," Eldon said. "Just grab some clothes and a sleeping bag. We'll get some coffee and couple of breakfast burritos on the way out. 7am, here?"

"Yeah, that sounds great," Matt said, as he packed up his harps.

37

AMY PARKED HER truck after her shift, gathered her bag and her tips, and buzzed herself into the building. Rachel was still up.

"Hey, Rach," Amy said, "What are you doing up?"

Amy was glad to see Rachel reading on the couch. It was nice to have someone to come home to for once. Amy flopped next to her.

"I'm beat," she said. "Good tips, though," pulling a stack of bills from her bag. "I need to get to bed. You OK here on the couch?"

"Um, sure," Rachel said, "this is great."

Amy kissed Rachel on the forehead and went to her room. She was almost asleep when she heard footsteps in the hall. Rachel pushed open the door and stood at the edge of Amy's bed.

"What's up, Rachel?"

"Well, um, I was wondering if I could sleep in here with you. Nothing weird or anything. I just feel really safe with you. If its OK, I mean. I'll squeeze over to the side."

"Sure hon. But I gotta warn you, I'm a pretty good snorer."

It used to come more often, even once a month in the first year or two after that day. Now, some version maybe once or twice a year. It was that day by the creek and Amy stood, looking over the edge, down through the thick alder brush to the bottom of the ravine. She knew she should run but she was frozen there, willing her legs to move to no affect. Something, someone was crawling up through the thicket. With raspy, gurgled breathing, clawing at the dirt and rocks came he up through the devils club. His fingers were bloody and torn from the climb and his long greasy hair was tangled with leaves and sticks and thorns, matted with blood. The right side of his face was crushed in from Amy's blow and the rest of his body was twisted and broken and bleeding as he looked into her eyes, each handful of dirt bringing him closer. But it wasn't Darrell, it was someone else, or maybe both of them but it seemed less like a dream and more like a premonition and it was but then it wasn't devils club, it was blackberries, at the back of the parking lot of some club and she was caught in the vines, the thorns ripping at her skin as she tried to get free and then it wasn't Darrell at all, but someone else, someone she knew but couldn't quite make out. Finally he would reach out and pull her down.

Amy came back to this plane, her own bed, thrashing and then it was Rachel reaching out for her.

"Amy! Its, OK! Its just me."

Rachel had her own version of this dream, she could see it in Amy's eyes in the dim light, she pulled her close, holding on for dear life until Amy stopped shaking and they both slept.

Across the street, a man stood in the shadows, looking up at the apartment, a phone to his ear.

38

Eldon queued up the Stone's *Exile on Main Street* and skipped to Stop Breaking Down as they hit the I-84 East under a leaden sky. He touched the wipers every couple of minutes to push off the mist. On the edge of the Columbia River gorge they pulled off at Troutdale, with its massive truck stops, like some kind of terrestrial space port. As travelers left the metro area the travel center had everything to cross the vast space of the west. Fuel, showers, a chapel and pornography, chips and jerky, smokes and 5-hour Energy drinks. People far from home or on their way to a new one or no home at all, with their hand lettered signs standing by the exit, Stuck, Need Gas Money. Mostly blank faces, tired, bored, humorless. These are liminal places, where no one lingers. This was touching down, filling up, and getting back on the road with some combination of road burn and caffeine. Some underfed, but mostly overfed. But whatever it was this was not a happy place. An acre of food that would eventually kill you, assaulted by the light, the colors, the sounds walking among the true citizens of these places, the truckers, moving plastic shit no one needed but everyone bought and soon threw away so some other trucker could haul it to the landfill. The truck drivers seemed to come in two sizes, with nothing in the middle.

Meth skinny or fast food grande. The big ones got down the road with 64 oz Big Gulps and chicken strip dinners, with a large fry. The skinny ones on something more compact, and even less nutritious. The rich, the upper middle, they didn't stop at these places but had their own cocoons with organic snacks and artisanal light roast coffee drinks in their cup holders. They might get gas at one of these foreign outposts but stayed in their vessels, peering out at the denizens, like a thousand other versions spread across the continent.

Matt and Eldon made their way to checkout with mugs of bitter coffee and greasy breakfast burritos.

"I got this," Matt said, pulling out his wallet.

They left the truck stop and the interstate towards Hwy 26, Mt Hood and beyond, out to the desert. It was a word most folks don't associate with Oregon, a place synonymous with rain and grey. But past the Cascade range, which caught much of the moisture, annual rain fall fell to single digits in some places. Matt dug into his harp bag, the rattle of the plastic harp cases muffled by the old leather, and pulled out a small woven bag with a drawstring. From it came a cylinder of metal and plastic, about the size of a pencil. Matt pressed a button on the side and a small LED lit up. Cannabis was so convenient now.

"Mind if I hit this while we're driving?," Matt said, holding the vape pen towards Eldon. "Want any?"

"Naw, I'm good for now," Eldon said. "Knock yourself out."

Matt took a hit and Eldon turned up the tunes, now on to Samantha Fish, a stunning and crazy good blues guitar player from Kansas City, then Larkin Poe, two sisters out of Knoxville. Sister Megan's slide work was enough to make you weep. After an hour or so they crested the pass among massive fir trees and headed down towards the Warm Springs Indian reservation, the trees changing from fir to pine and finally open grass land and sage brush. Now past the rain shadow of the mountains, the weather had gone from gray and damp to dry and warm, even hot. The cannabis took charge now, in a benevolent but insistent way and Matt watched the scenery fly by, mostly in silence, until he surfaced for a moment.

"Hey, Eldon. OK if we stop soon? Wouldn't mind something to drink and maybe a bag of chips or something. There's that market in Warm Springs, just down the hill from the gas station."

"Okey, dokee."

They left the highway for the rez market and a different world. Some would say the third world. The rates of poverty and substance abuse were obscene with little help from the outside, white world; a kinder sort of genocide. The community had recently endured a 10 week boil-water ordeal when the city water system failed with no funding to fix it. In any other part of the state a 10 week boil-water situation would have spurred near panic. But here, it was just another indignity to add to the list.

They pulled off the highway and down the hill to the market. A taco truck sat across the parking lot, a hand-lettered sign advertising Carnitas and Fry Bread. Eldon waved a hand in front of Matt's face.

"Hey, you in there, buddy? You want some taco's?"

"Yeah," Matt replied, "grab me a couple I'll go inside and get us some water."

As he stepped from the air conditioned Chevy the light and the heat smacked him like a bat. It had been misting and fifty eight when they left Portland that morning. Now, midday, in the rim rock canyon, it was well over ninety, the air bone dry. A few locals were sitting on the front curb and took note of the Impala and nudged their mates, nodding approvingly. Matt nodded to the enrolled tribal members and pushed through the door while thoughts rushed past him, quick revelations, metaphors and sound bites bouncing off, reverberating with the surroundings. And while he had been through here many times, back and forth to the fleece, down jacket and Pinot Noir communities of Bend or Sunriver, the circumstances of his adjusted state created an off balance reality. In a meandering and uncertain arc through the market, beyond the chips, soda and canned beans, Matt found himself among a set of glass cases containing a decent collection of tribal artifacts, documents and photos. He could hear the hum of the store in the background, the beeping of the cash registers, greetings of the customers, the bell at the door but as he looked at a set of artifacts his mind wandered into them. A stone bowl and pestle, some wood and bone fishhooks, items of everyday use pulled him in, made him wonder about the lives that were led here. Not some simplified version of the noble savage but an attempt to think about their actual lives. Lives at certain human level weren't much different from his own - love, hate, jealousy, longing. Thoughts ricocheted around his head, some landing on a branch to sing their brief song before flying off into the blizzard in his stewed brain. Now somehow at the cash register, Matt paid for the water along with a spontaneous assortment of sugary things and crunchy salty things and emerged from the market, blinking and wobbly. The place had unmoored him a bit, that this existed in his state, and that his people had done this to these people, were still doing it to these people. The same three men sat as before. Overweight, dealing with the symptoms of the poverty, alcoholism, obesity and diabetes. Matt thought he could see the actual weight of it on them. The first two ignored him, more important thoughts to dwell on. But the third fixed Matt with unblinking eyes, as if trying to discern this strange pale creature before him. Matt wanted to put some sort of importance to the moment, to the man. Maybe the staring presence was trying to tame its own a meandering stream of thoughts - hope *money for beer?*, curiosity *you look a little clean cut and pale for around here, except that you're as fucked up as I am* and general disdain *fucking whitey*. Matt shook free of the man's gaze and watched as Eldon carried a greasy paper bag from the taco truck. Matt greedily wolfed the first taco as Eldon pulled out of the parking lot towards the highway. As they left, an older but otherwise nondescript sedan at the back of the lot started its engine. It waited for a moment before pulling out and joining Eldon's Impala on Hwy 26 east. They climbed out of the Deschutes Canyon, passing south through fields and pastures, small towns and commercial strips, through Madras, Redmond and Bend finally turning left just south of La Pine, to the southeast toward Lake County. Now off the main highway, few cars going either way, Eldon pushed the speedometer to eighty while Matt took another hit and melted into the seat. Too stoned to do much about it, it occurred to Matt that Eldon had gone quiet, staring out the front windshield, his face unreadable. Climbing up and over Picture Rock Pass, the Summer Lake playa was spread out before them. The lake itself, an alkali remnant of a massive Pleistocene inland sea, occupied the foreground. But most of what they could see was a desert playa of several hundred squares miles, framed by sage and juniper mountains, in a pallet of grays and tans melding perfectly with the unbroken blue sky, so utterly alien to the west side, with its dense fir forests, blackberry thickets and emerald green fields.

"Whoa," whispered Matt.

"Yeah," Eldon said, "don't really ever get tired of that."

The Impala descended along the lake bed, the pool table-flat playa on their left, the three thousand feet of basalt cliffs and scree of Winter Ridge to their right. Between them and the mountain proper was a low angled bench of land, maybe a mile deep, of pasture, hay and grazing cows. They passed a rusted gate.

"You can't quite see it," Eldon said, "around the rise of that hill, but that's the place, up that dirt road. But we'll head into town for supplies first."

They had crossed the great expanse of sage and rimrock got to Paisley in a fog. Well, a fog for Matt anyway. Outside his head, it was cloudless, dry and hot. Inside his head, well, maybe he oughta just stay in the rig while Eldon gets the food and beer.

"Here," Matt said, "pushing a couple twenties into Eldon's hand. I think I'll just chill here."

He pondered the view outside the car window, not noticing the dusty sedan parked in the shade of a large cottonwood across the highway that served as main street in Paisley. He saw boots, ball caps, and pick-up trucks adorned with any number of second amendment and Trump bumper stickers. He loved this landscape, and there were good people out here. Git shit done kind of folks. But in others, men mostly, the anger was like a faint glow. Mad at the government, at the environmentalists, the liberals, the Mexicans for taking their jobs, the rich bastard that closed the mill — and maybe sometimes at themselves for not having the courage to leave. The ones that were smart enough, or brave enough, they left. But it was home and those that left almost always wished to return. But here were the holdouts, distilling themselves in the echo chamber of the local tavern. Eldon was probably right that Matt not advertise his origins. Suddenly Eldon was beside his window, with a couple of grocery bags and some ice.

"How about a hand here, ace?," stirring Matt from his reverie.

The groceries stowed, Eldon slid into the driver's seat.

"Alright," he said, sliding into the driver's seat, "let's get to the ranch."

Neither said a word on that long straight back to the gate. Matt climbed out and swung the gate open. As they rounded the hill and the ranch came into view, it was not an inspiring sight. A beat up double-wide trailer along with a couple of outbuildings and a barn, all needing paint and much more. Next to the barn was a disused paddock, dried cow pies among the thistles and pounded earth.

"Well, shit," Eldon said. "Don't this look like hell."

Matt agreed but stayed silent, this being Eldon's childhood home and all. They walked around the property and it didn't get any better. The trailer looked like hell, maybe it was a meth lab, maybe the last tenants were too lazy to get even that far.

"Jesus," Matt said, "what do you do with all this? Where do you even start?"

"That's a great question, Matt. Not sure I know exactly. But we ain't doing much tonight," popping the trunk and pulling out two beers. "I'm sure as hell not sleeping in there either. But that's cool, it'll be an amazing night for stars. We'll sleep out in the sage."

Eldon hoisted the grocery bags, handing one to Matt. "Let's get a fire going and cook those steaks. You brought your harps, right?"

The talk of steak and beer and jamming seemed to clear their moods as Eldon dug in the cooler ice.

"See if you can round up some wood," Eldon said, tossing Matt a can.

"On it," Matt said, pulling the on a second beer.

Somewhere around a six-pack each and midnight, the coyotes began their song. Matt's eyes moved outside the firelight.

"Ah, hell," Eldon said. "Don't worry about them. Coyotes don't eat people. That's how they survived so long. But if you're worried about it, just take a piss near your bag and mark your territory. Ain't nothing out here going to bother us."

39

PEG HATED MATT on nights like this, with what he called his black belt in sleeping except he wasn't there to hate tonight, on some kind of desert mission with his new best friend. And it wasn't just the waking up because other nights she would wake without the damn engine running. Those times were frustrating but not harrowing. No, it was the waking sense of dread, like some dark form sitting on the edge of the bed that got her. She felt it as a thing and had given it a name, the Anxiety Engine. She'd drawn pictures of it as an intricate sort of steam engine, about the size of a toaster with small brass gears, belts, miniature little drive chains, busily whirring away, a little smoke stack, puffing. Whatever thought went in came out black and awful. Commiserating at 10am over the third cup of coffee with another insomniac, it almost seemed funny. Alone at 3:37am, not so much. And so tonight she got up. Might as well get some work done, maybe grab a nap later. She opened the shared laptop and waited for the browser to come up, then clicked the 'history' button looking for that NIH research site. Among the New York Times, ESPN and Cooking Network links was another set, maybe a dozen, all starting with www.pdxsaucygrls.com\amy\. She paused, a little twist in her gut, and before thinking if she really wanted to do that she clicked on \amy\photo1. A young woman, short blond hair, pretty enough, not wearing much clothing or make-up. Tired and wired at the same time, sort of like watching herself in a minor car crash, she clicked through the others finally clicking on \amy\message. Peg stared at the blank form page and the blank form page stared back and she clicked on the last link: \amy\club_schedule.

That afternoon, the rusted wire of no sleep taut in her head, Peg's car sat wedged between a plumbing company pick-up and a late model Honda with a baby seat in the back. She could go in the club but that seemed awful; enemy territory so she watched the men come and go. They were like most men she saw in her day - blue collar, white collar like the pick-up and the Honda. A few caught her eye, looked away quickly, and Peg smirked, *I must remind them of their wives*. Others with curiosity. Maybe a dancer waiting for her shift or a prostitute? Jesus, what the hell was she doing here anyway? I should be talking to Matt, not staking out a strip club, she thought. But as she reached to turn the key, the side door of the club opened and out stepped the woman in jeans, t-shirt and flip flops, carrying a gym bag. Fuck it, Peg said, stepping from the car.

"Hey, um, Amy?"

Amy looked up, wary, then with the barest smile.

"And you're Peg," she said.

"Huh?"

"Matt showed me your picture," Amy said. "Wanna get a cup of coffee? You probably didn't come to catch the show. Know the Ugly Mug on 13th?"

"Uh, sure," Peg said. The wire lost a bit of its ting.

They pulled out of the parking lot and Peg's sedan fell in behind Amy's rig, a full sized Ford pick-up and Peg thought that's not what a stripper should drive, then thought what would a stripper drive anyway, then thought a strip joint on one block, a fair trade coffee joint on the next and finally wished that she'd gotten more sleep before doing something like this.

Mid-afternoon, except for a few hipsters with ear-buds, the place was mostly empty. The barista put down her copy of *Polyamorous: A Vegan Guide* and slid off her stool.

"What can I get you guys?"

With coffee in hand, and paying separately because really what was what the etiquette for coffee with the wife and the stripper maybe mistress, they took a table. It looked like Amy hadn't thought this far ahead and Peg hadn't thought much at all since 4am and so a dense little cloud formed between them. Finally, Peg looked up, pointed her chin towards the barista, a row of bottles on a shelf up behind her.

"Fuck it," she said. "You want a beer?"

"God, yes," replied Amy with something like relief and Peg's wire unwound a bit more as she went to the counter. The etiquette still unclear, so no clinking of bottles. Just a nod to each other and a long drink as the air in the room started to find some balance. Peg tore a strip from the label and looked out the window.

"Listen, I don't even know why I'm here," she said. "I feel like an idiot. But I didn't sleep last night, and he, we, well we're really not getting along very well I'm just trying to figure out what's going on."

And Peg thought she was going to cry and so she stopped and took another long drink of her beer.

"Listen, Peg. Matt's a nice guy. We mostly just talk. I think he gets some kick out of hanging out with a stripper. But mostly we talk about music and real estate. And you guys."

"What do you mean, mostly?," Peg said.

"Oh, gee," Amy said, working on her reply. "Guys like to look at naked young women. Its how I pay for my houses. Most of them are lonely. Some of them are jerks. He's not one of the jerks. I know you guys are trying to work some stuff out. I'm a good listener. And he gets to see me with no clothes on. But he seems like a good guy, Peg. He's not really guilty of anything other than being too chatty."

"Listen, Amy. I know Matt's been looking for Rachel, with his new best friend. The cowboy PI he calls him."

Peg could see that Amy was thinking, like she wasn't sure how much to tell her.

"Listen," Amy finally said, "I know you and Rachel were close. So yeah, she's been staying with me."

"Oh gosh," Peg said. "How is she? So glad she's off the street."

"Well, she's dealing with some serious shit. But I'd better let her decide what she wants to tell you."

"I get it, Amy. Please tell her I love her. I'd love to see her if its OK."

So they drank and talked and Peg cried a little bit and Amy let her and they finished their beers and Peg thought seriously about a second one. She had come to the club to confront the stripper maybe mistress. Now she felt like giving Amy a hug. And punching her husband right in the nose.

40

JEFFREY USED TO have meetings like this in some dark bar. Cory had offered to teach him how to use the web anonymously, but Jeffrey was not a digital native and had always preferred cash anyway. Cash wasn't traceable and as long as he left his phone off, Jeffrey wasn't either. Although, with the ubiquitous security cameras, meeting in some quiet bar wasn't foolproof anymore either. If you wanted something done right, or more rightly, discreetly, you did it yourself. So as the dust settled on the hood of Jeffrey's 7-series BMW, he sat parked among 20-year Fords and Chevys and Toyotas in the back of the rutted parking lot for a strip joint called the The Fallen Princess. Where did they get these names anyway?, he thought as he sent a text.

out front

A couple of minutes later the passenger door opened and Cory, with his particular aroma, slouched into the leather.

"Don't worry Jeff," Cory said. "I'm not fucking your wife anymore. I know better than to mess with a rich guy's pussy. Besides, she was like sleeping with a box of staples. I like 'em with a little more meat on their bones."

"Be careful," Jeffrey said. "I could have you arrested with a phone call."

"Cut the bullshit, Jeff. I could have your house burned down with a phone call. Get the fuck over yourself."

Jeffrey eyed Cory for a moment before laughing quietly. Cory stared back.

"What's so funny, Jeff?"

"Oh nothing," handing Cory the envelope.

"Remember," Jeffrey said, "no trace."

41

MATT SURFACED FROM a dream while Eldon stirred in his bag. Light flickered on his eye lids as he rolled awake. The trailer was engulfed, flames and sparks climbing into the night sky. Eldon put a hand to his arm, Shh, he said, pointing left of the burning trailer. Someone, a man, stood watching the flames, eyes wide, transfixed. Against his thigh, he held a pistol.

"Hey wait," Matt said. "Isn't it?"

"I believe it is," Eldon replied. "What the hell is he doing out here?"

Finally, Randy turned and walked down the dirt track, around the bend and out of sight.

"He thinks we're in there," Matt said.

They heard Randy's car fire up, a glow of headlights heading towards the highway.

"And he was going to make sure we didn't come out," Eldon said.

They watched the trailer burn, transfixed.

"Well," Eldon said, "let's make sure this fire's not going anywhere. Then we'll roll at first light. See if we can figure out what's going on."

It was near first light when Randy got phone service close to Silver Lake. His phone pinged with a voice mail. A message from one of his dealers. It's amazing how observant they can be with a couple hundred dollars available.

"No fucking way," Randy said out loud, dialing a number. "Both of them?"

"Cory, it's Randy," he said. "No, no, it's all good. A two for one, in fact. That prick from the alley was with him. But, hold on. You're not going to believe this."

42

MATT WOKE TO the acrid smell of the smoldering trailer. Eldon's bag was empty. Matt climbed out of his own and stood, surveying the scene. The sun was just up, already hot and piercing. Eldon stood with a cup of coffee, studying the smoking pile. Twisted shards of metal jutted out of the blackened rubble. Noticing Matt, Eldon held up an empty cup.

"Morning," Eldon said, handing Matt a steaming mug. His eyes were on what remained of his childhood home.

"So," Matt said, "what the hell was Randy doing out here? And why the trailer with us in it. Seems like a long way to go for a grudge."

"Yeah," Eldon said, "I'm inclined to agree with you there. We'll have to work on that when we get back to the city. It'll be a bit easier considering he thinks we're dead."

More silence and more coffee.

"Jesus, Eldon. I'm sorry."

"The SOB probably did me a favor," Eldon said. "Should have done it myself years ago."

Eldon pushed the dirt with the toe of his boot.

"Might as well get out of here," he said.

They loaded the car and surveyed the scene one more time before heading out. When they picked up cell service Eldon hit Amy's number. It went straight to voice mail.

"Hey Amy, I'll explain more when we get to town. But you might want to keep your eyes open, both you and Rachel. Not sure what's up but one of Cory's pals paid us a visit last night. Call me when you get this."

The miles passed in silence, worry not far below the surface, until Matt spoke up.

"So," he said, "you don't have to answer this. But you said Randy might have done you a favor. How'd you get from here to Memphis anyway?"

"Well, Matt," Eldon said, rubbing the side of his face while he stared down the highway. "That is a long story."

The trailer shuddered in the wind and Eldon, twelve by then, stared at the television, willing himself into the screen. Outside the trailer, the high desert of eastern Oregon, it was fifteen degrees and blowing thirty. The circle of light from the flood lamp high on the barn was swirling with snow. The pick-up, half in darkness, just visible on the other side. Behind him, over him, his mom and her boyfriend Jimmy screamed at each other. To say "the latest fight" wasn't right. It was all fight now. Jimmy had never hit his mother, not so much as you'd worry anyway, but Eldon could see something building behind his eyes.

Eldon Truly was born in 1976, in Lake County, Oregon, near a tiny town called Paisley, where his father was from - eastern Oregon high desert country. Sage brush and rimrock, bunchgrass, wind and sky. His mother Connie was from Memphis, working at Arnold Air Force base near Tullahoma, where she met Frank, stationed there during the Vietnam war. Frank's parents had passed before Eldon was born, a combination of old age and orneriness and he never knew Connie's father, dead early from too much whiskey and barbecue. All he remembered of his grandmother, a big woman in a faded cotton dress, was a warm and smothering embrace that smelled like biscuits and fried chicken. After Frank's discharge, they moved back to the small family ranch outside Paisley. They were going to make it on their own in the west. And for the first few years, it was good, his parents were young and shining, building a life and those years had the colors of the wide blue sky and the high prairie with friends and big barbecues where someone would do a whole steer, a monster on a spit to Eldon, dripping grease into the juniper coals. This was cowboy country after all, a beer in every hand, the whisky bottle making the circle. Sure there was fights, but mostly over nothing, just young bucks rutting with a handshake after. But over time, with the mill closing, it all got too hard and those fights were still about nothing but with fewer handshakes after. And the shine, the brightness, began to leave his parents, especially his dad. Too many times in the circle. So when Eldon was six, and his father died out hunting alone one day, they called it an accident. Everyone knew that's not what happened and not much more was said. But Eldon and his mother tried to make a go of it, with and without a series of boyfriends, Jimmy being the latest. His memories of this later time, leading up to that last night, have a washed out feel to them, the colors dull and muted, like an old Western, the kind where the good guy doesn't always win.

Eldon thought maybe if he stayed very still, kept his eyes on the screen, he could keep the balance, keep it from breaking. If he could stop breathing, stop time, he would.

But it was too much and he watched Jimmy push Connie to the couch and scoop up her purse. He dug around coming out with the pick-up keys, jangling, and a fist of bills.

"I'm going to town," he said.

"Jimmy, stop it, you'll never make it. Plus we don't have any money, that's the last of it."

"Fuck it, I'm going to town."

He swung on his coat and pushed the door open as wind and snow swirled into the trailer's front room. Leaving the door wide, he stepped off the porch into the ankle deep powder and made his way to the truck. She leapt from the couch, into the storm, after him. Eldon jumped from the floor and stood at the doorway. His mother was on Jimmy's back and he spun around, trying to throw her like a two legged bronc. Jimmy, stop it, you can't go to town, she said. He finally shook her off into the snow. As they looked at each other, no sound but the wind, an emptiness yawned between them. She reached up, snatched the keys and threw. All three watched as the ring of keys, sparkling among the snow flakes, arced through the light and out into the darkness, as gone as if she'd dropped them in a well. Connie got her feet.

"That's it, Jimmy. Let's get back inside."

A strange and flat light came to Jimmy's eyes. Later, Eldon could put words to it, to Jimmy's decision. He was trapped here now, truly trapped, and he would punish his captor. As he laid into Connie, fists and boots, she gave right back. But he was too big, too angry, too much and she fell back to the snow. And then Eldon had the shotgun in his hands, the one they kept by the front door for the coyotes. He screamed for Jimmy to stop, to leave her alone.

Jimmy looked up, and stared at him with the same flat gaze. Eldon got some idea of what it meant and pulled the 12 gauge up, pointed at Jimmy's chest. But there was too much weight, the gun, the task, and he let it drop. This was the moment that stuck with him, that still ate him alive at three AM. Why hadn't he pulled the trigger then? Why did he wait? Ignoring the weapon, Jimmy's eyes left Eldon and set back to work, the boy paralyzed on the porch. Satisfied with his work, Jimmy stepped over the form at his feet and moved towards the next chore, the boy. As Jimmy reached for him, Eldon drew up the 12-gauge and pulled the trigger, both triggers, tumbling back from the kick, with an image, branded to his memory, of Jimmy cartwheeling out of the light in a red mist, spun away by the wind. The boom still ringing in his ears, Eldon scrambled to his mother, snow already drifting around her. He was never quite sure how they had made it inside or when, somewhere down the county road, the wind had taken the phones and the power with it. The darkness and the storm and the pain pushed down on them and he made a nest of his parent's bed, piled with blankets. They were both child and parent that night, holding each other, like when he was little. A promise was made, a pact.

"It will be too hard for you," she said. "They won't understand, not here, his folks are from here. Promise me this, please promise me, tell them I did it."

They made their promises and then she started to slip away, talking in turns to her mother, a young Eldon, his father before they finally slept.

He woke to light flooding the room, hard and white, and no sound but his breathing. He held her still body and cried, for her, for all of them, until there was nothing to do but get to town. The storm had passed but it was somewhere near zero. He bundled up and opened the front door to pure whiteness; windless, silent and impossibly bright. Eldon stepped off the porch into the glare. After he made it to the highway, then to town that frigid day, his memory was a fog of sheriff's deputies, DAs, CSD case workers and hearings, finally clearing in the warm, humid air of Tennessee and the fresh biscuit smell of his grandmother's hug. She stepped back, hands on his shoulders, and took a long look. Beside her stood a lanky Black man, about her age, gray at the temples.

"Eldon, this is Curtis."

The man smiled and held out large hand, and they shook, man to man.

"Pleased to meet you, Eldon. Welcome to Memphis."

"Damn, Eldon."

"Like I said," Eldon replied. "A very long time ago."

Twenty more miles of silence. Matt pulled out his phone, hit a number.

"Hey babe, it's me. Wait, what?," he said. "Amy? You met her?"

But then the call didn't go the way Matt thought it might. They signed off a few minutes later.

"I love you, too," Matt said. "I'll let you know when we hit town."

43

THE MORNING SUN shone through the kitchen window of the apartment. Amy was making her coffee when Rachel padded in, rubbing the sleep from her eyes.

"Morning, hon," Amy said. "Get you some coffee? There's some bagels and cream cheese plus whatever you can find in the fridge. I need to check on some contractors today. I'll be back about lunch. Maybe some Thai?"

"Sounds awesome." Rachel said. "Beats dumpster diving."

Amy pulled on her work jacket and shouldered the tool bag.

"Hey listen," she said. "Thanks for being there last night. It happens once in a while. I'm sorry if it freaked you out."

"Oh, no," Rachel replied." I'm super glad I was there."

"And," Amy said," you'll get to meet Darcy, my bartender pal. I've got the day shift today. She's going to give me a ride in. Saves me some parking."

Amy planted a kiss on top of Rachel's head and scooped up her keys.

Amy made her rounds and, Thai food on the seat next to her, parked the truck back at the apartment. Turns out that Rachel was growing on her. She'd forgotten how it was to think about someone else. She kind of liked it, in spite of herself. She had her keys out but the door was ajar. She started to push open the door and saw Rachel sitting on the couch. "Hey hon," she said, "I got us some lunch."

Rachel sat stock still, staring across the room. Opening the door all the way, Amy followed Rachel's eyes.

"Hey babe," Cory said, a smirking Randy at his side. "Let's go for a ride."

When they'd reached their destination Mike's voice came into Amy's head. It seems he'd left her with one final lesson.

44

THE IMPALA WAS passing through Madras, about half way home, when Eldon's phone rang. It was Darcy.

"Fuck," she said, "I'm freaking out here."

"Slow down Darce, what's going on?"

"They're gone, Eldon. Both of them."

"Who's gone? What do you mean they're gone?"

"Amy and Rachel. They're gone. I was supposed to give Amy a ride in today. But when I went by her place, the door was open. Her truck's there, her phone and purse, everything. Except Amy and Rachel. And shit's knocked over, Thai food all over the living room. I'm fucking worried Eldon."

"OK, Darce," Eldon said. "We're on it. Hang in there. You know Amy's a tough one. Let me know if you hear anything and I'll do the same."

Eldon hit Betty's number.

"Afternoon, E," she said. "How's it going, young man?

"Not good. Betty, listen. We got a problem," he said. "Rachel and Amy are missing."

Eldon told her as much as he knew, or thought he knew.

"Hold on, Eldon. I'm taking some notes," while he told her about the call from Darcy, and Randy and the fire.

"I'll call Tony," Eldon said. "But don't know what to tell him. A supposedly missing stripper and street kid isn't going to get us very far. Not quite sure what's going on but I think there's a connection between Cory Stalmers and our client Jeffrey. Jeffrey's not going to get his hands dirty so I'd start with Cory.

After he hung up with Betty, Eldon dialed Tony. He paused, pressed End, and put the phone down.

An hour later, Eldon's phone rang.

"Hey there, Betty. Got anything, sweetheart?"

"Not much. But three addresses have Cory's name attached. All in SE. I'll text you the addresses. I'll see what else I can find and call you back."

Eldon made a couple of calls including Mel. More for something to do, they sure as hell weren't going to be downtown. Eldon pushed the speedometer to eighty-five. The miles flew by and they stared out the window.

"What about Jeffrey?," Matt said.

"Yeah, I guess you're right," Eldon said, reaching for his phone. But as he scrolled to the number, the one for Jeffrey's burner phone, Eldon knew. Jeffrey wouldn't answer, would never answer because he didn't want Rachel found. Eldon had been played and Rachel might already be dead. Amy, too. Collateral damage. It hit him like walking into a meat locker.

45

BY THE TIME the Chevy hit Portland in the early afternoon Betty had sent a half dozen possibilities. They had talked on the phone a few times, parsing the odds. Eldon hung up from the last call and sat for a moment, looking out the front windshield.

"Hey Matt, I'm dropping you at your place. No need to get wrapped up in this shit. Besides, I might need you for something else."

What Eldon didn't say was that he didn't want to have to look out for Matt's sorry ass, too. Matt gave a mild protest but let it drop. When they got to Matt's Eldon reached over to shake his hand.

"Hey Matt, thanks for listening. Really."

"No problem," Matt said. "Sure I can't do anything?"

"Naw, I think I'll take it for now," Eldon replied.

"But keep your phone close. We might need you yet."

As Matt turned towards the house, Peg was standing on the porch. They wrapped themselves together as the Impala rounded the corner and disappeared.

The first house was in Rockwood, a sprawling suburban nowhere between east Portland and Gresham. As Eldon pulled up the street he knew this wasn't the one. A one-story ranch, small but well kept. A landscaping rig was in the driveway, its trailer full of yard debris, while the hispanic owner sat with a beer, laughing with his wife on the porch while three kids kicked a soccer ball. Eldon texted Betty

rockwood's out. anything else?

Ten minutes later three more addresses pinged on his phone. Three more strikes. It was towards dusk but at least the traffic was easier now. Eldon had made some more calls and Betty had sent a couple more addresses. Nothing. And in his gut, the same feeling. The feeling as he watched Jimmie beat his mom in the snow. The same helplessness.

Another call. Betty.

"OK," she said, "This one looks pretty good. Its a big, old house on flag-lot off Holgate. It backs up to Johnson Creek. The lot's pretty overgrown with an apartment between the house and the street. Owned by guy a named Wilson Crenshaw, taxes all paid up. And that's all fine except Mr. Crenshaw is doing three to five at OSP Snake River for robbery and assault. From the county records, it looks like Cory's picking up the tab. Luckily, the sat photo's pretty recent with a few cars parked out front including a blue Mustang which resembles a car owned by one Cory Stalmers. I did a term search on the available case records and Cory's name pops up a couple of times. Maybe he's house sitting. I'll text you the address. Just head for the 120's on Holgate."

Eldon pointed south, then east on Holgate, weaving through traffic. He swung off the avenue and sped down the driveway, gravel and dust flying as he slammed to a stop in front of the house. Maybe a hundred years old, it had probably been the farmhouse for the bottom land along the creek, before it filled up with houses and apartments and strip malls. The windows were filthy and dark. Paint was peeling from the house and ivy climbed its walls. What was once a grand yard was now an overgrown thicket. It seemed no one had been here for a very long time.

"Fuck!," Eldon said, slamming his fists on the steering wheel. Nothing, another dead end. He got out of the car and climbed the porch, straining to see through the dark and silent windows. Deserted. Now what? Maybe downtown, a vague plan to beat it out of Jeffrey, like that would work even if he knew where they were. Eldon started the car and pulled on the headlights. As he swung the car around something caught his eye, a glint, through an overhanging laurel hedge. He stopped the car and pulled a flashlight from the glove compartment. Walking towards the hedge he caught a couple more sparkles and a hint of color. He pushed back the branches and there it was. Cory's blue Mustang. OK, then, he said quietly. Eldon took another look around the house and under the ivy, found the entrance to the original root cellar. And maybe recent footprints. Along the door, old wood with rusted but well oiled hinges, he could see a slim shaft of light. As he pulled open the door the light went out and he heard Amy's voice.

"Eldon! No!," before his own lights went out.

What Eldon didn't see was the small webcam tucked in the ivy. Amy was talking to Rachel, who had fallen into a kind of comatose state, something she learned from home, something many victims learn. To take their mind somewhere else while their bodies are used by another.

"It's OK, hon," Amy said. "We'll figure this out but I need you here with me. We'll need to do this together."

Rachel stared at the floor in front of her, her face blank, unmoving. Then the lights went out and she heard Cory chuckle.

"Come to papa," he whispered. Now there was only candlelight and she saw Eldon's face appear in the doorway. She screamed but it was too late. Cory brought the baton down on Eldon's head. As he groaned awake, a cuff ratcheted down, the other end attached to a chain in the basement wall.

When they'd left the apartment Cory's Mustang was in the back alley. Rachel and Amy were blindfolded and stuffed in the trunk. A half hour later and stumbling down a set of stairs, the bandanas came off and they'd found themselves in a basement, maybe thirty feet square. Besides a couple of stained couches and soiled bedding, there was a large work table covered with the tools of Cory's trade. Scales and packaging, food wrappers and beer cans plus a couple bottles of whisky and a few large candles. Cory pushed the women to the far side of the basement where drain pipes ran down a moldy concrete wall. Rachel had already drifted away but Cory needed Amy to pay attention and do what she was told. As he screwed the muzzle into Rachel's temple, he told Randy to grab two pair of handcuffs from the table.

"Cuff her to the pipe and make sure they're tight," he said. "I do not trust this bitch. Then get this one."

Mike's voice came into Amy's head. They'd been sitting around the fire, Mike just back from brief stint in the Lane County jail for chaining himself to a bulldozer. Between protests, tree sitting and the occasional drug bust, Mike had experience with law enforcement accessories.

"So, Amy," he'd said, "here's the thing. They like to crank 'em down tight. You'll want to open your palms, facing up, then make a fist, hard. That'll make your wrist bigger and they won't bite as much."

So as Randy pulled open the cuffs she flexed, feeling the rush of blood through her shoulders and arms. As he leaned in behind her she added a last touch, one that wouldn't help his concentration.

"I want to blow you," she whispered.

"Sure, babe," he said standing up.

But she'd felt him flinch.

After he finished cuffing a silent and pliant Rachel to another pipe Cory told him to get lost.

"Ah c'mon, Cory. I to get want some of this," he said."

"Don't worry, Randy. They're not going anywhere. But you need to make your rounds. Its collection day so get the fuck out of here," Cory said.

All the while, Amy was flexing her wrists and arms, testing the cuffs.

A grumbling Randy had made his exit and Cory stared, silently, at his spoils. He lit the candles, one at a time. He looked at the small flames and back to Amy.

"Really sets the mood don't you think?," he said.

Next, he dug around on the cluttered table and cleared a spot for a broken piece of mirror. Pouring out some white powder, he cut himself a few lines on the glass. He snorted a line, took a drink from the whisky bottle and did another. And while Rachel sat mute, Amy started in on Cory.

"What the fuck, you prick, like you're going to get away with this?," she spat. "This how you get off? Can't get a girl to fuck you otherwise, you gotta chain 'em up?"

Cory put the whisky on the table, walked over and struck her across the face.

"Shut the fuck up," he said.

She could feel her eye swell, blood running down her cheek. Despite the handcuffs and blood and the pain, her mind held one thought. He will die in this basement. She didn't know how but she knew. For now, she attached herself to the pain and worked her left hand back and forth, the skin stripping away, blood flowing, dripping from her fingers. As she worked her wrist, she spoke softly to Rachel. But then the lights went out and she heard Cory.

"Come to papa," as Eldon's face appeared in the doorway and she screamed.

With Eldon firmly attached to his own piece of rusted metal, Cory took a deep breath and turned towards the women.

"Alrighty then," he said, "let's get this party started."

She watched as he attached large shop lights to a couple of tripods. To another tripod, he attached a video camera. Satisfied, he turned everything towards Amy and Rachel and plugged in the lights. Brightness flooded the basement as Amy squinted into the glare. Cory glanced over at Eldon.

"We've even got an audience this time. Hope you enjoy the show Eldon," he said. "I've got folks that will pay plenty for this."

Cory snorted another line and tipped the whisky bottle back, pushing things around on the table, looking for something. Her hand slid free of the cuff and the sound of Darrell hitting the bottom of the ravine came into her mind. Cory held up a piece of cloth, black with colorful printing. A Mexican wrestler's mask. He pulled it over his head, touched Record on the video camera and walked into the light. Keeping her hands behind her, Amy pulled in her legs, as if kneeling in supplication. Cory stood in front of her, his breath slow and shallow, one hand tipping her head back, the other reached for his zipper. Amy leapt, a shoulder in his chest. She drove him to the floor, Cory's ribs cracking to shrieks of pain as they tumbled apart. Cory was hurt, hurt bad, but the drugs were making up the difference. They stood at opposite ends of the large table and Cory rooted around and held up a knife. Amy reached for the baton, the one Cory had used on Eldon. As they circled each other, lunging and darting, he caught her in the side as she swung the baton into his left side, deep into the shattered ribs. Now lost in a cloud of drugs and rage and pain, Cory rushed Amy and threw her into the table, with the drugs and the scales and the whisky and candles crashing and tumbling onto the rags and bedding strewn on the floor beyond. Despite the rank dampness of the basement, the bedding caught, smoke filling the room. But Amy and Cory saw none of this, each too focused on the other. Eldon was yelling, trying to distract Cory while Rachel continued to stare silently, her mind far, far away. Amy entered her own kind of blindness and waded in swinging. She dodged a couple more arcs from Cory's knife and caught him along side the head. This one connected and Cory fell, landing on his back. Then she was on his chest, gripping the empty cuff, pummeling his face. The fire grew but she only saw Cory, the blood roaring in her head, as flames climbed the wall. Then there was something else, a voice. Mike, like at the creek.

"Amy! Amy!"

But it wasn't Mike. It was Eldon.

"Amy! Stop! He's done, we need to get out of here."

Like before, she came back to herself, chest heaving. Blinking, she looked around. Cory, his face a bloody pulp, was inert but still breathing while Rachel, unmoving, laid against the far wall. Against the nearest wall Eldon called out.

"Amy, get the keys. His pockets," he said.

She fished the keys out and freed Eldon, then Rachel.

"OK," Eldon said, "we gotta go."

The smoke and the heat were almost unbearable as they felt their way up the stairs and into the night. The last one out, Eldon pulled the door closed behind him and tumbled into the grass along side Amy and Rachel, gulping air. As before, once she was clear of the danger, the adrenaline welled up and Amy threw up in the bushes.

"You ok, hon?, Eldon said. "We gotta go."

"Yeah, I know," Amy said, coughing, pulling her arm across her mouth with a deep breath and a shudder. "Ok, let's get out of here."

"It's OK, hon. We're out. Its all gonna be OK," she said, her arm around Rachel.

"Listen, Amy, we need to get her out of here. This place in going to go. We need to get in the car now," he said.

Cory had done a thorough job sealing the basement and no sign could be seen of the fire, not yet anyway. But, with three stories of dry wood and tar paper above it, that wouldn't last long. They turned onto Holgate, flames already licking out the first floor windows.

46

AMY HELD RACHEL in the back seat and as the Impala traveled west. As they left Holgate for McLoughlin Blvd the Willamette River and downtown came into view. The lights of the city skyline shimmered in the calm river, Jeffrey Barton's building among them. Son House played in the background, Death Letter Blues. Rachel was still silent while Amy and Eldon hadn't spoken since leaving Cory in the burning house.

"Pictures," Rachel said.

Amy sat up, "Huh? Did you say something, hon?"

"Pictures," she said again. "He took pictures. I think there were others, too."

"Jesus," Amy said.

They were silent again.

"I think I know where he keeps them."

Amy and Eldon talked some, Rachel nodding. The action, the forward motion brought her back to herself. Soon there was a plan.

"You sure, hon?," Amy said. "This will get you right out there, no more hiding. I just want to make sure you're clear on what's coming."

"Fuck yeah," Rachel replied. "Just wish I could go with you."

"OK then," Eldon said. He scrolled to Matt's number while Amy placed her own call.

"Matt, hey," Eldon said. "Yeah its all good, they're both in the car with me. Yeah, yeah, they're OK," he said, glancing in the rear view mirror at Amy's wrist, wrapped with some laundry from his trunk. The wound in her side, while not too severe, leaking into her t-shirt.

"Well, pretty much OK," he said as Amy, her own phone to her ear, winked at him. "But listen, remember when I said we might need you? Got a pen? I'm going to give you some directions. Its kind of hard to find."

One final call to Betty, "Betty, it's Eldon. You did it. Amazing. Yeah, yeah, we're OK but can you send me everything you can find on, what's the address, Rachel?"

He hung and caught Amy's eye in the mirror.

"All good?, he said.

"Yep," Amy replied. "She's waiting."

When Eldon's Impala bumped over the bridge to Jadie's place, Matt's sedan was already parked in front of the house. Jadie sat with Matt and Peg on the front porch, candles flickering on the table between them. As they climbed from the car Peg jumped from the porch and Rachel, finally letting it all go, fell into her arms sobbing. Amy gave her mom a hug. But soon Jadie was all business.

"C'mon, Amy," she said, "let's get you cleaned up. We're wasting dark."

Eldon put an arm around Matt. "OK, here's the deal," Eldon began.

Thirty minutes later they were all back on the porch. Matt, Peg and Rachel sat close in the porch swing. Jadie gave Eldon another one of those kisses, then touched the end of his nose.

"You watch yourself," she said.

Rachel repeated a four digit number and Amy wrote it on her wrist.

"You still OK with this, hon?," Amy said. "If this works, shit show doesn't begin to describe it."

"Fuck yeah," Rachel said. "Just don't forget to hit 'pound' after the numbers."

47

WHEN THE OLDER neighborhoods of Portland were built in the 19th or early 20th century, horses still provided much of the hauling. Iron rings were embedded in the curbs. An early form of emergency brake. Now they mostly sat as historical artifacts, doing nothing but increasing the value of the nearby real estate. Except for today. As Simon Wheeler, a retired bank president, walked his wife's old and tiny dog in the half light of the June morning he saw a shape curled on the sidewalk. A shape that from a distance looked like a large, hairless dog. But as he got closer, the shape became a person, a man.

Jeffrey sat bound, gagged and naked; chained to a horse ring. Attached to his body, with duct tape wound around his pale, paunchy belly was a plastic file folder marked: Detective Tony Mason, Portland Police Bureau.

AUTHORS NOTE AND ACKNOWLEDGEMENTS

The title comes from *Death Letter Blues* by Son House. A staggering work. Just him and that resonator guitar. As Curtis put it, the voice of God.

For all the other things this book might be, it is also a love letter to Portland. Warts and all. But, anyone familiar with the city will notice a few things. Many, if not most, of the establishments in the book are no longer there. Covid, Fentanyl, and the summer of 2020, and all that followed took its toll. Others, like Mary's Club, aren't in the same place. Some places never existed at all. Matt and Jeffrey's building, for example. And Jadie's place. But Portland was, and remains, a great city and there are no alleys in Old Town.

Thanks to Dardi Troen for the coolest cover ever, Beth Everett for all things author and Lara Heber for her editing help. Also thanks to Liv Østhus for her help with Amy. Finally, thanks to Charlie and Jack for being awesome.

Alan Hickenbottom is a native Oregonian who has been accused of never traveling outside the bio-region to which he pleads mostly guilty. He doesn't see the point.

9 7 9 8 9 9 9 1 7 2 1 9 2 9